THE SELKIE'S LINEAGE

Loren Cruden

Copyright © 2012 Loren Cruden

All rights reserved.

ISBN: 1477514694
ISBN-13: 978-1477514696

DEDICATION

For my ancestors and grandchildren

ACKNOWLEDGEMENTS

The Selkie's Lineage is a fictional tale but includes real places, people, and events: the Great Sheep Drive and the Highland Clearances, as well as dramatic events in Ireland and Skye during the Land Wars, are actual.

Trinity and Connell and their families are invented, as is Rona/Fionaghalla. Their stories are woven into those of historical characters. For instances, in the Greenyards battle I substituted Duncan Ross for a man named David Munro, who, it was reported, flung a constable five yards before being clubbed unconscious.

Thanks to Aonghas MacNeacail for permission to use a verse from his poem *Sireadh Bradain Sicar*. During research I was given invaluable help from Janette French at the Gairloch Heritage Museum, and from the staffs at the Michael Davitt Museum in Straid, County Mayo; Skye's Highland Council Museum Library in Portree; and Clan Donald's library in Sleat. The almost magical ability of librarians and archivists to receive my questions and pull from the shelves exactly the references needed (without using computers) was dazzling. At judicious intervals, those wizards also quietly set books on my worktable answering essential questions I hadn't yet formulated.

Many thanks to Rob Kerr for alert proofreading and skillful suggestions, and for bringing indigenous sensibilities to bear on a newcomer's literary incursion. All errors or modifications of facts are, of course, my own: apologies for irresistibly slipping a few Lowland colloquialisms into the mouths of Gaelic-speaking Highlanders.

The texts listed in the partial bibliography helped me with details. The author whose vivid descriptions I drew most heavily on is John Prebble. His popular writings about Scottish history are forthright and accessible.

Lastly, I'm grateful to family, friends, and husband for my life in Scotland; to the people who helped a stranger with the kindness so enduring in Scottish temperament; and to the generous power of the land itself in telling its story and making me feel part of it.

THE SELKIE'S LINEAGE

PART ONE

Partial to men in kilts, Trinity Ross arrived in Scotland to be confronted with scarcity, male Highland knees unexposed, Gaelic pride and practicality shadowed by southern pretension and the smell of extinction.

In Edinburgh, she craned her neck at castle cliffs with déjà vu's vertigo, as though having scaled those walls in a previous existence. Her eyes instinctively sought routes up unyielding pleats of rock, hands twitching as though recalling bloody nails, slick night dew, jammed knuckles. Not her imagined sense of homecoming.

She had flown from America to London, at King's Cross boarding a train to Edinburgh, arrowing into a history she hoped would subsume if not reconceive her.

"Will you go to Easter Ross?" her father had asked—her sonless old man stonewalling the past but having a bard's memory for genealogy. Where else but Ross? She heard her father intoning notes on the family scale of lineage—sons of sons: Neill, Donald, Duncan, David the immigrant with his son, Murdoch. Then the North Americans: Duncan, Donald, and John—Trinity's father—who ended the song by having only a daughter, though one who kept the Ross name, a where as well as who.

Trinity leased a car in Edinburgh and drove north to a hostel in Ardgay, on the Dornach Firth, the cusp of Easter Ross and Sutherland, where blue waters resolved into sheep and cattle pastures. Green slopes curved upward into moorland, and the river Carron shouldered through stands of birch along the strath's rocky basin. It was peaceful despite early April's shiver, bracken steepled and brown, wind furrowing the firth's cold face.

The hostel was beyond the village; a converted stone schoolhouse surrounded by sheep, neighboring a stone church with a goat tethered in its walled yard. The long strath extended past the hostel, quiet, smoothed by wind. Sheep and red deer browsed among ruined blackhouses, where Trinity's ancestors had lived. But the strath seemed devoid even of memories, so utterly had its brood of inhabitants been swept away.

On a Friday in late July, 1792, the Strath Rusdale Rosses celebrated a wedding with the customary music, dancing, and home-distilled whisky. In an atmosphere conducive to expansive schemes, a particularly bold plan took shape from the heady alchemy of kinship and whisky fumes. The Rosses decided to call for a foray to free their lands and souls from the flood of imported Lowland sheep the lairds had brought to the Highlands. The Rosses would restore ancestral well being. They would drive the invaders from Glen Achany, Strath Oykel, Strathcarron, and Strath Rusdale, south to the Beauly Firth and on to Inverness. The call would go beyond Ross to Sutherland, and perhaps even inspire the men of Inverness to extend the drive, relaying sheep shire to shire until the Highlands were purged of the Cheviot menace.

The call was answered. In July's kind warmth, the sheep were moved. Clanspeople watching them pass called cheerful encouragement to the drovers. The herd flowed south, the air pierced by bleating protestations and the terse commands of shepherds directing ardent, scurrying dogs. The men were businesslike but defiant—resolve born in rock and tireless wind, in peat-dark cold running rivers, in centuries of sword and summoning fire.

The lairds, gathered in Dingwall by Sheriff MacLeod (and, between the twenty-three of them, owning all the land in Ross-shire) were in a panic. Skating over the root of the problem—their avarice—they resolved that rationality and law would prevail.

Meanwhile, the Great Drive unfolded, flocks surging through Ross, a tide of more than six thousand sheep. The four hundred men accompanying them halted the herd at Boath in a valley seven miles from the Cromarty Firth. It was August fifth. That afternoon, three companies of the Black Watch arrived in Dingwall at the disposal of Sheriff MacLeod.

Neill Ross was twenty-five in the Year of the Sheep. He lived his life in Strath Rusdale much as his father had, which was little different from how Ross clanspeople had abided for centuries. It was true they could no longer fish for salmon or hunt the grouse and deer. They were also forbidden timber for building and barred from carrying arms or freely grazing their beasts. It would not be many more years before tenants would only be able to work, worship, or marry according to their lairds' dictates. But in 1792, Neill Ross still conversed in Gaelic, affectionately tended his cattle, grew oats and potatoes in runrigs, and drank whisky illegally distilled by his neighbor and kinsman Diarmid Ross.

Neill was deceptively strong, more cunning than wise, especially at twenty-five. He possessed responsiveness rather than ambition. The responsiveness pooled in Strath Rusdale. It was sensitive and land-intimate, its back to the larger world, which was felt as an occasional finger of derisive wind against Neill's spine. Catherine, his wife, was a Munro from nearby Strathcarron but had an almost foreign softness that, though pillowing Neill, ill suited survival's rigors. She bore Neill a daughter; a second was born in the Year of the Sheep. On hearing the call for the Great Drive, Neill went eagerly with his kinsmen.

The soldiers of the Black Watch plodded behind the horses of Ross-shire's gentry, led by Sheriff MacLeod. The intention was to fall on the drovers camped at Boath, but those drovers, getting wind of authority's approach, took to their heels, abandoning the sheep. MacLeod and his troops vigorously searched the glens for two days, and twenty drovers were hauled from fields and homes and arrested. Most carried the name Ross. Five were designated by Sheriff MacLeod as ringleaders and charged with "advising, exciting, and instigating persons riotously and feloniously to invade, seize upon, and drive away from the grounds of the proprietors flocks of sheep amounting to several thousands," whereby "a daring insult was offered to the law, the public peace was disturbed, and the property of the lieges greatly damaged and at the mercy of a lawless and seditious mob."

The laws of property had been violated, though in the eyes of The Highlanders their acts were attempts to recover surpassing rights more sacred, natural, and antique. The sentences passed on the offenders were staggering, varying from lifelong banishment to impossible fines and imprisonment. Temporarily lodged in the Inverness jail, the prisoners were freed one night by an unknown sympathizer and not heard of again.

Neill Ross, among the drovers, eased a cautious route home when word came of the soldiers' proximity. Eluding arrest, Neill resigned himself to the reinstallment of Cheviot sheep and the constant reminder their presence gave of how little the Gaelic way of life, and the Gael, were valued. It ate at his self-respect, and his wife's softness became an anxiety into which, three years later, their third child—Donald—was born, and Catherine died.

Trinity turned from contemplating frisking lambs. Dark water squelched beneath her hiking boots. She dallied along a lane lined with dry stone walls, breathing the damp messages of soil and wind, a daffodil innocence. A man stood at the head of the lane, his back to her. She slowed, but the man heard her, pivoting like a gunfighter whose coolness gives superior advantage. Trinity veered, startled. The man doffed his cap, a disarming gesture.

"G'morning," Trinity said, poise holding against a jostling gaze. He made no answer. A smile's sunbreak—light, not warmth—rode her to the hostel door.

"He's Northern Irish," the hostel warden told her that evening in the kitchen.

Trinity fried potatoes, paperback tucked under one arm. She was washing up when she heard his step, knowing without turning that it was not that of the St. Andrews student or one of the young German cyclists. She heard him plug in the electric kettle. Pulling a warm dishtowel from the radiator, she began drying her plate.

The nearness of his voice made Trinity flinch as he asked pardon, could he please get a cup from over the sink. She looked at him, then, dignity in capitulation.

"Connell O'Sullivan," he said. "Care for a cup of tea?"

In 1820, the jaunty young laird of Novar directed his factor to clear the tenanted estates at Culrain for the grazing of imported sheep. The strath was rich and green, slopes rising from the sheltered valley floor through which rolled the river Oykel. When Culrain's five or six hundred clanspeople about to be evicted in favor of sheep heard of their fate, the tenants—who had never been arrears on rents despite inexorable increases—offered to pay more. But a Lowland sheep farmer had agreed to a price beyond what the tenants could match, and, in February of 1820, Writs of Removal were served.

At Culrain, an army of forty police, twenty-five militia, and a host of local gentry and their retainers faced a substantial crowd of shouting tenants—mostly women, with a scattering of men positioned behind the roadway's stone walls. Neill Ross, now fifty-three and a widower, was not there. Neither was his son, Donald, whose wife was pregnant. But both Neill Ross' married daughters were in the crowd at Culrain when old Sheriff MacLeod came brandishing Writs of Removal.

The rising tide of evictions, occurring as they did strath by strath, took advantage of insular communities and lack of organized resistance. For centuries, Highlanders had relied on benign paternalism's understood reciprocities. There was no mindset among clanspeople for dealing with betrayal by their own chiefs.

Sheriff MacLeod's efforts to disperse the gathered people in Culrain rapidly degenerated into confrontation. Constables and gentry laid about with bludgeons and riding crops, striking women who retaliated with stones. The militia fired. One young thug ignored the order to use blanks: his lead shot tore through a woman's chest. The sheriff and his men made haste to escape, leaving MacLeod's carriage to be trashed by a mob that pursued police and gentry to Ardgay, hurling stones and imprecations at the forces barricaded within the Ardgay Inn. Abruptly, it was over; the tenants thought their point made and thought it sufficient.

The voice of the church was employed to undermine resistance in the straths. Ministers were rewarded for applying their terrifying religious leverage, a graphic message of damnation for those who defied the law. Reverend Alexander MacBean delivered this message in Strath Oykel—implacably, morbidly, until tenants, beleaguered to the soul, accepted the writs.

Connell explained that he was in Ardgay between "bits of business" in Inverness. "Lodging is cheap here, and I like the quiet," he said.

Trinity noted his vagueness over what otherwise was a clean-featured landscape, and, capriciously, was drawn. Connell's Irish accent charmed her. His hair was black, his skin fair as sea-foam, his eyes dizzyingly blue: she fell for him as Deirdre had fallen for Naoise—precipitously. In the sheep-trimmed grass above Culrain they made love, in mid-April when midges had yet to punish such exposure.

Lying in the lee of a boulder, cushioned by heather, Trinity's jacket beneath them, Connell's above, Trinity gripped Connell the way roots quest stone to find nourishment from what seems impenetrable. Connell's sexual knack was an instinct bypassing calculation, as though skill was an impulse born of sensitive hands. After their first coupling, Connell asked Trinity if she was Catholic.

"No," she said. "Does it matter?"

He shrugged. "Your name."

Trinity shifted, sat up, drawing Connell's jacket around her. "I was conceived during a camping trip in California's Trinity Alps," she said. "My parents were famous for outdoor passions."

"Ah, well," he said. "Lineage tells."

Frequently during the following three weeks, Connell left "on business," Trinity unquestioning. Their relationship existed in a selectively conducive medium, discernment's commentary muffled by desire's clarity. Trinity had no living relatives in Easter Ross, but walked the grassy straths in search of a connection that gradually lost any focus but the walking itself. The moors simplified experience—though nothing about them was without dimensions of intricate, sometimes tricksterish, power. In this walking she would forget Connell, only to find, on return, a calmly ferocious hunger for him. As though the land itself, if not the solitary walking, incited an urge of procreation.

Strathcarron, extending westward from the Kyle of Sutherland, divided into three ravines, each with its burn that fed the dark waters of the river Carron. The four or five hundred people living in Strathcarron were mainly Rosses and Munros, populating the strath's two estates: Greenyards and Glencalvie.

In February of 1842, the laird's factor, James Falconer Gillanders, began the process that would empty Strathcarron of its people.

THE SELKIE'S LINEAGE

Duncan Ross, grandson of Neill Ross, lived on the Greenyards estate with his wife, Annie, and son, David. Though only twenty-four, Duncan was well regarded in and beyond the township for his easy but principled character, his astuteness in matters of cattle and clan, and his fine good looks. Duncan's wife regarded him highly as well, for qualities making marriage a place of contentment. Annie MacBeath, no great beauty, had never expected courtship from a favorite like Duncan Ross. But her severity in repose only heightened her grace in motion, and a stamina neither stoic nor spiteful.

Life in Strathcarron was shadowed by uncertainty as the lairds of Sutherland and Ross burned houses and swept clanspeople to the world's fringes like ashes from an ancient hearth. The Rosses of Strathcarron clung to normality, but no longer did their clan chief embody normality's holding center. Duncan and Annie, like their neighbors, moved uneasily in this miasma. Both everyday toils and celebratory releases were infiltrated by impending loss. The people danced on a precipice and did not—could not—look down.

Their *sennachie*, blind John Chisholm, saw the past with vivid precision. He calmed his listeners around flickering peat fires, drawing aside the curtain—always diaphanous in the Highlands—veiling the past. He reminded them of five hundred years of Strathcarron Rosses, of clashing feuds with MacKays and MacKenzies, of the swift-kindled sacrificial courage of the Gaelic race.

He didn't, however, recall to them the debts of the last Celtic Earl of Ross who, in the 1700s, caused ancestral lands to pass to Charles Ross, an unrelated Lowlander of Norman lineage. And the sennachie had not the sight to prophesy that it would be 1903 before the lineage of the Celtic chiefs would be reinstated, too late to really matter. The storyteller's vision illumined a long season of complex, introverted history. But it was a gaze with no imperative to penetrate the murky future, where the gaze itself would decay in irrelevance.

Trinity had slipped outside her life's orderly momentum. Its tangent to Scotland now lost itself in context, as moorland paths become lost in bog and the deceiving sameness of braes. Relationship with Connell was not so much an orientation as something of glimpsing insight. She went to him as to a scrying pool whose surface in certain moments is mirror still. He could hurt but not disappoint, for she had yet to form expectations. She went to him as she did to the moors. "You are beautiful," she said, and he was, but feckless, as though scorning potentials for profit.

For all his magnetism, Connell shied from interactive depths as though not wanting to be memorable. They avoided the trafficked hostel bunkrooms, made love in temporary nests of bracken and heather, or in mossy hollows of the birch wood. Sometimes, they were interrupted. It was hasty sex, Connell resentful at the gypsy quality of their love life. Details mattered: ground must be held.

When Connell was away, Trinity returned to herself, a cooling in which doubt stirred. She walked to outpace it, looking for landmarks that might complete her, make her substantial, though these kinds of connections in Connell's life seemed to harry rather than make him whole. One day she hiked the long road past Glencalvie to the old Parliament church at Croik, where she wandered among the graves, reading the names of the dead.

In 1843, the church at Croik emptied, all but two of Gustavus Aird's parish families following their minister out of the Established Church—tool of clearance lairds—into the Free Church. For Aird and his parishioners, this meant Sunday services held on an open hillside. The Free Church was vigorously opposed by the lairds. In Sutherland, such churches were forbidden. Riots ensued, and the military intervened.

In the year following Aird's bold move, Glencalvie's factor summoned the township's rent payers to a meeting—giving the impression new rents were to be discussed—then handed the assembled tenants Writs of Removal. The Rosses were caught by surprise and without their staunch women. They were given until the following spring to vacate the township—if they promised to plant no crops.

The extra time was no mercy: in a year, Ross families still had nowhere to go, no resources with which to build new lives—and no harvest to sustain them. Dread did not delay spring's arrival. Glencalvie's tenants expected compensation for their stock and resettlement elsewhere in Ross-shire. Instead, each family was handed £18 and advised to emigrate.

May in 1845 was particularly rainy. Glencalvie's snug cottages stood silent and smokeless, devoid of the life that had existed there for centuries. The township's inhabitants huddled in the churchyard at Croik, sheltering beneath rugs, plaids, blankets, horsecloths. The Glencalvie Rosses were now refugees like thousands of other clanspeople in the Highlands, worth far less than sheep in the eyes of the lairds.

The Ross clan chief, with a seldom-used home near Glencalvie, said nothing when his people were expelled from their ancestral lands. The evicted families occupied Croik's churchyard for a wretched week, then disappeared to fates unknown. The only response to the chief's betraying silence was scratched by his cast-off folk on the window glass of the church at Croik: *Glencalvie people were here....*

Trinity pressed her finger against the diamond pane on which Ross names and messages were cut. The phrases were in English. She hunched deeper in her jacket, thinking of kinswomen in their red shawls partitioning makeshift tents with blankets, trying to create decency amid wind and slashing rain, shamed by eviction—though rents had ever been paid, proudly exact. *Glencalvie people the wicked generation*, one desolate Ross had scratched on the church window.

Trinity turned into the wind, rain on her cheek. Nearly May, and the wind cut, even through fleece and nylon. Trinity walked out the iron gate of the churchyard. That night, she lay awake on her bunk, having the dorm room to herself, imagining emigrant ships: tainted drinking water, stink of corpses among the living, dark holds packed to twice their designated capacity. The strath's emptiness opened in Trinity's mind, an unnatural wilderness.

She shifted onto her side, and in the dark heard the door open, felt Connell's presence, said his name.

"I got back sooner than planned," he said, glancing around, for once no other occupants in the room. "Were you asleep?" Warm palm smoothing her hair, fingers tinkering with her nightshirt buttons.

"I was thinking about clearance immigrants sailing to North America in slave ships."

Connell's hand stilled. "Fares from Dublin went as low as twelve dollars, they were so eager to get rid of us," he said. "The real price paid by the poor is always in flesh and soul, their pocketbooks being so thin. Divine punishment for the sin of existence."

"Did any of your ancestors emigrate?"

He picked at a splinter in the bunk railing, shrugged. "The ones I know about are the ones that stayed. In Mayo, Dublin, Belfast. Stayed to fight—and get fucked over. Generation after generation."

Trinity touched his hand, he jerked away. "Spare me the patronizing."

She raised herself on her elbows, stung. "I'm not trying to steal your suffering. I just want to understand what happened. Those were my people."

"Understand what happened?" He snorted. "What about what's still happening?" He turned to go. "You Americans and your tender sensibilities."
"Why do you despise me for where I was born, for the life my ancestors made?"
He paused in the doorway. "Don't take it personally. It's not about you."
"But it's about you?"
He opened the door.
"Wait."
He stopped.
She said nothing.

Trinity took day trips into the far north, land furred with green like the velvet of new antlers. Narrow lochs glimmered between the hills. She explored among broken curves of *brochs*, unmortared stones held by the weight of centuries. Nothing here was entirely opaque, despite this weight. Not stones, not peat; no compression could overcome the porousness of history.
In the northern light, aliveness was apprehended without assumption. Anything could happen. Sheep and deer droppings were modest messages of survival, as once had been the tracks of the land's human inhabitants. Trinity walked miles in that space, permeated with a sheerness of light and silence. When Connell entered her, he entered luminosity.
Their relationship eddied in this transcending physicality. It was not that it lacked more ordinary intimacy—or perhaps it did, in its resistance to personal or social narrative. Its intense privacy was like a third entity, the place where they met and perfectly joined. To speak of it was to argue, stumble, misunderstand. Trinity knew too little and Connell too much. It rendered them both incapable of explaining themselves.

When Trinity attended a *ceilidh* with Connell at the Ardgay village hall, she was caught in a state like that produced by reckless tippling. She skipped and swirled, hair flying as Connell swung her in tight circles, his steady grip holding her to the hot grace of his body.

Four hundred people populated Greenyards, including the family of Duncan and Annie Ross, though, as in neighboring Glencalvie, only four names appeared on the rent books. With Strathcarron stripped and desolated of its people, and now Glencalvie cleared, the factor turned to emptying Greenyards. But the Greenyards women did not wait for writs and evictions to catch them unaware. Early in 1854 they posted children to watch on Ardgay hill overlooking the road from Tain and on the drove path from Alness.

Greenyards' tacksman, Alexander Munro, surreptitiously met with the factor and the laird's law agent to plot the delivery of removal writs. Despite secrecy, the meeting was known of in Greenyards. A party of Rosses appeared at Munro's house asking for assurance that evictions were not in the offing. Inviting heaven to judge him if he lied, Munro swore he was innocent of issuing removal warrants. Duncan Ross, who had instigated the call on Munro, heard this declaration with skepticism.

At age thirty-six, the astuteness so evident in Duncan as a youth had well ripened. Duncan's fine-tuned ear that caught, exact, a fiddle note or the vibrations of his wife's mood, detected falsity in the tacksman. "You swear the rumors aren't true?" Duncan pressed, and the sweating Munro again called upon Divine powers to bear witness to his oath. But Munro would not meet his questioners' eyes. Duncan turned away unsatisfied.

At home, Annie waited in her chair by the hearth. Young Margaret had fallen asleep in the season's early dusk. David, fifteen, fidgeted on the long bench, ostensibly repairing a pony halter. Excitement broke rein at his father's entrance. "What did he say?"

Duncan halted inside the door, hanging his coat on a peg and glancing at Annie before sitting beside his son. "The tacksman swears he didn't authorize eviction warrants."

Annie lowered her knitting to her lap, revealing pregnancy's rounded landscape. Two babies had been lost: the infant son born eighteen months before David, and the miscarried daughter four years after David. Then had come Margaret. Annie smiled, self-deprecating, fending concern. "The rumors are false?"

Duncan was silent a few moments. "Alexander Munro did not convince me," he said finally, "and if he is lying, God help us."

It was not yet day on Friday, the 31st of March, when thirty-five constables armed with muskets and truncheons tramped to a rendezvous with Sheriff-substitute Taylor of Tain. With the Ross-shire official were the procurator fiscal and the laird's law agent. The constables were liberally provided with ale, porter, and whisky, and, after binding themselves to an oath to take no food until the women of Greenyards were punished and subdued for their refusal to accept Writs of Removal, they were exorted to have no mercy on the disorderly females.

While constables fortified their resolve, the females of Greenyards moved about with homey morning chores, well being re-created each dawn in smoke rising from peat fires, in the nurturing smell of porridge, the splash of warm milk in chill tin pails.

On that last morning of March, the flow of tasks was interrupted by the sudden shrilling of the lookouts' whistles. Women straightened from hearth and milking stool and peat stack, jarred by adrenalin's twisting surge, but externally calm: life-giving bodies must stand between well being and what would destroy it. The women could not indulge despair or afford the foolish hopes of their men—their obsolete faith in chiefs or their ingrained horror of public disgrace. Celtic women ever have known paternalism's flaws. Women in Greenyards laid down domestic implements and walked from cottages, some gathering stones as they walked, holding them in their aprons like potatoes for the midday meal.

In Duncan Ross' cottage, Annie froze, hand poised to wipe milk from her daughter's face. She completed the gesture, set down the cloth, and rose. Duncan already had his arms in his coat when he turned and saw the set of Annie's face.

"No," he said. "Think of the bairn inside."

"I am," his wife answered. She drew her shawl around her shoulders, turning to David, who had also risen. "You bide and watch over Margaret." David clamped his jaw; no more was said.

Sixty or seventy women gathered to block the brigade of constables. Fewer than twelve men joined them, clenching sticks, standing behind the women. The crowd waited silently in the chill, overcast morning. The women had scarlet shawls drawn over their heads; several clutched closed aprons that sagged with stones. A few, like the men, gripped sticks.

The rumble of Sheriff-substitute Taylor's carriage was loud in the stillness. The carriage rolled to a stop in front of the gathered women. Taylor, the fiscal, and the law agent alighted and stepped to the fore of the cadre of constables. In Gaelic, Taylor shouted for the women to open a way for the law.

No one moved. Taylor took a copy of the Riot Act out of his pocket and began reading it to the crowd. Christy Ross, wife of one of the four tenants in the rent book, pushed forward, interrupting Taylor. "Alexander Munro, our tacksman, denies issuing removal warrants!" she declared, drawing out Munro's letter to the laird stating this denial of authorization. At Christy's movement, the crowd pressed forward; Taylor angrily turned to the constables and ordered them to clear a way.

Fifty-year-old Christy Ross was promptly bludgeoned by three constables. As she fell, they drove nailed boots into her face, breasts, and shoulders. More constables rushed forward. Elizabeth Ross' frontal and parietal bones fractured under a blow ripping open her scalp. As with Christy and the other women felled by batons, Elizabeth continued to be beaten once on the ground.

Elizabeth's sister, Janet, charging to her sibling's defense, was likewise cudgeled. A third sister, Margaret, was stunned by two blows and dragged away in irons. Another Margaret Ross resisted with her fists and fell under repeated blows. Constables followed as she sought respite under a thorn bush, kicking her head until she crawled out. One officer knelt on her breasts, dragging her hands up, his partner clamped on handcuffs.

Most of the crowd tried to flee the wave of violence. Placid Ann Ross, an unmarried woman of fifty-six, suffered blows to the head; her elbow snapped; her gown was shredded. Margaret MacGregor Ross, whose seven children anxiously waited at home for their mother's return, crumpled, her skull mortally shattered. Sturdy Ann Munro, a second cousin of Duncan's, wrested the truncheon from one attacker's grasp, heaving it into the Carron, casting herself after it as three constables rushed at her with raised batons.

The river was sanctuary for Grace Ross as well. That timid girl was beaten until unconscious, then battered again when she regained her senses and stumbled to the river, her blood staining the waters. Young Naomi Ross' breasts and vulva were slashed by nailed boots. An uninvolved neighbor, hearing screams and moans, forded the river, ripping bandage strips from her apron. Two constables intercepted, clubbing her back and shoulders until she collapsed into the river and was carried downstream.

Annie's closest friend, Catherine Ross, was seized and beaten while trying to help her neighbors. She struggled, fighting back. A constable smashed her head with a stone, then knelt on her breasts to handcuff her. His cohort, believing Catherine dead, dissuaded his comrade, and they abandoned her. Regaining consciousness, Catherine dragged herself into sheltering bushes.

Of the men, only two—and two brave boys—stayed to fight. Donald Ross, a Waterloo veteran of nine battles, fared little better than the women. Duncan, planted beside his wife, was attacked by three constables. Truncheoned on the head, half-blinded by streaming blood, Duncan seized a constable around the waist and flung him aside before two others clubbed him senseless. Thus Duncan was spared the sight of the blow that killed his gestating daughter.

Duncan and four of the women: Margaret Ross, twenty-five; Margaret Ross, eighteen; Christy Ross, fifty; and Ann Ross, forty, arbitrarily were designated the incident's ringleaders. They were manacled and hauled to the Tain jail in a cart. Removal summonses were executed on the bloody field, then Taylor and company repaired to the Ardgay Inn for refreshments. Twenty women and girls were severely injured, but people outside the strath could not believe the ugly reality; it sounded too lurid.

With Gustavus Aird's help and that of a doctor arriving to treat the injured, the so-called ringleaders were released on bail after two days in jail. The constables had come away with no reported injuries. The Greenyards' tacksman continued to deny complicity, though his name, indeed, was on the warrants. Newspapers refused to print accounts differing from the conviction that authorities never permit unnecessary violence. Their reports chastised the Greenyards women, saying that whatever happened was undoubtedly instructive and deserved. Tenants were expected—even by those sympathetic to their plight—to be submissive. The

Lord Advocate refused to investigate the actions of the constables, though Margaret MacGregor Ross lay dead. Ann Ross and Duncan Ross were charged with mobbing and rioting, breaches of the peace, and assault on officers of the law in execution of their duty. Realizing the savage penalties faced, they agreed to plead guilty to lesser charges, though this meant no trial, no exposure of the truth. Ann Ross was put in prison for a year. Duncan was sentenced to eighteen months' hard labor, leaving his bed-ridden wife in the care of neighbors, all evicted twelve months later.

After his fourth trip south from Ardgay, when Connell informed Trinity he was returning to Ireland she didn't react neutrally, trivializing her feelings and behavior. Neither did she cling. Connell, hitchhiking north to Ardgay, was outside Conan Bridge when Trinity had happened along. He swung himself into the car, laconic as usual, making his announcement.

"When are you going?" she asked.

He rolled a cigarette, cranking open a window. He didn't look at her; the hand holding the cigarette moved from lips to denimed thigh, where it rested a few moments, lifting again. "Soon."

Trinity could think of nothing to say. The car rushed along the neatly winding road, past pastures of sheep and cattle, past stone walls, churches, farms, and flashing burns. Connell's hand raised and lowered, smoke loitering around him with all the time in the world.

"You could come partway if you cared to," he said, the absurdly hopeful reluctance. "As far as Glasgow, if you like. Have you been to Glasgow?"

"Glasgow," Trinity repeated. "Why that far and not to Ireland? I'm not asking to go, just asking why. Is there a wife?"

Connell looked startled, grunted a short laugh. "No wife." He pinched the end of his cigarette against his boot sole and flicked the stub out the window. "I guess there's no point in your coming to Glasgow. I just thought...." He grimaced. "Fuck it. You once told me that sex was enough. Now the questions. Let's leave it sweet at Ardgay."

"Sure. Leave it at Ardgay, but don't carry on like I've violated some pact. What is it with you and your bits of business, anyway?" she asked, despair's recklessness. "Is it some kind of IRA stuff?"

The tension beneath Connell's pallor suddenly drained, revealing a fatigue beyond sleeplessness. "Never ask," he said.

At the hostel Connell got out of the car, slinging his duffle over his shoulder; they parted wordlessly in the foyer. Trinity retreated to her bunk, staring at the impersonal, Spartan room she'd occupied for a month. Her period was two weeks overdue.

She rolled onto her back, gently massaging her still-flat belly, sliding her hand under the waistband of her jeans. There had been no children in her failed marriage, no room for them in the space her husband had inhabited. "Wait until we have money," he'd said. Then, "Wait until we have the time." Now this. Connell with his, "Never ask."

She drifted to sleep fully clothed, on the merciful tide away from irresolvable argument. From time-to-time she woke, once fumbling out of her clothes without opening her eyes, dragging the duvet over her. Once with such blind need for Connell that she sat up, bent on going to him. But did not.

The MacKenzie lairds of Gairloch had been more philanthropic than many Highland gentry. Mary, wife of the twelfth laird, had urged employment of tenants to build so-called Destitution Roads during the potato famine. There had been few roads in Gairloch prior to that flurry of industry—and few actual clearances, the MacKenzies not being absentee lairds. That fact, along with the presence of Annie's

MacBeath kin, was why Duncan Ross found himself a fisherman on the fringe of Wester Ross.

He had been released from prison in October after serving his eighteen hard-labor months, endured as so much else was endured. Annie and the children had been taken in by the Gairloch MacBeaths after the Greenyards' evictions, Annie still convalescent from the violent miscarriage. Squeezed into a cottage already crowded with occupants, they later moved to the vacated North Erradale croft of in-laws who had emigrated.

Not only his family's circumstances, but the very core of family integrity was shattered on that day in Greenyards. Young Margaret alone seemed unchanged. Annie's graceful momentum had diminished to a gaunt, passionless trickle. She could risk no more childbearing. Marriage's sweet intimacy died.

David, now seventeen, had his grandfather Donald's lean energy and canny, secretive eyes. He flashed to anger and thinly forgave. The attack at Greenyards collapsed David's faith in his father's invincibility and his mother's wisdom. He was ashamed of Duncan's term in prison, flushed at the image of manacles and his father hauled away in a cart. He hated him for fighting and losing when other fathers had not fought. He hated Duncan's equanimity—that prison had neither degraded nor reformed the man David now strove to disdain.

Duncan was patient with this altered behavior, sensing but not dissecting its cause; patience that incensed David. More and more Duncan conceded to the mutual relief felt when David could be given solitary tasks. Only seven-year-old Margaret's twinkle kept family members, whose delight had been in each other, from drifting into isolation like lost planets.

So Duncan fished the waters of the Wester Ross coast and pondered how to heal his family. On a day of calm, almost flat sea, the morning humid—unnaturally still, so seldom does wind vacate the West Highlands—Duncan rowed alone. David cut peats on this placid morning when Duncan could handle creels and boat without his son's help.

Other boats could be seen, some venturing to try their luck near the Western Isles; most content with Gairloch's bay, its trove of cod and ling and glimmering shoals of herring. Duncan's eighteen-foot boat was more modest than the thirty-two footers with their four- and six-man crews. Fishing alone, he had to settle for lobstering or long-lining for cod. He was new to a place where the Ross name was not all that common. Alliances took time.

Near the mouth of the burn, the sleek, dog-like head of a seal broke the glassy surface. A fish arched in its jaws. Three gulls, vigilant for culinary opportunity, alighted on the water with mournful, clamoring demands—most self-righteous of beggars. Duncan rowed on, seeking his own catch. A weight of clouds subdued the dawn's watered colors. The oars creaked between their thole holding pins, water dripping in sweeping arcs on the bay's smooth surface as Duncan reached and pulled, an economy of effort learned from land work, applied to this new arena on which so much depended.

The boat coasted as Duncan scanned the wide bay with its humps of Eilean Horisdale, close by Badachro, and Big Sand's Longa, the old Viking retreat. The Isle of Skye dominated the horizon. Something anomalous floating on a kelp bed interrupted Duncan's traversing gaze. Too white to be a seal; too buoyant to be a garment.

His gut tightened. He pivoted the boat, pulling deeply on the oars. There had been no report of a missing person.... Sweat trickled into his eyes and down his ribs under his *geansaidh*. The boat slid across the gently breathing sea, slowing to a carefully maneuvered stop in the rippling kelp.

Duncan stared. His breathing snagged. A woman floated amid the kelp, eyes closed. He fixed on the rise and fall of her naked breast, the pulse, faint, in the hollow of her throat. Her russet hair spread in long curves as though adopted into the community of sea plants. She was half-submerged, supported by the kelp. She drowsed, it seemed, rocked in the sea's embrace.

Duncan leaned down and brushed her cheek with his fingers. She was deathly cold, and this broke his bemusement. He shoved ballast aside, knelt, and caught the woman's arm, drawing her toward him. Then grasped her under both arms and heaved her over the gunnel.

Water streamed, darkening Duncan's clothes. He laid her in the bow, covering her with oilskins. He chaffed her fine-boned hands and drew back the oilskin to listen at her cold breast: breathing, suspensefully languid. "Lady," he urged, tucking the oilskin around her again. "Wake now. Lady! Awake!"

The eyelids never stirred. She was elsewhere.

Duncan scrambled over gear, back to his bench, and began rowing hard. Never had the boat seemed so cumbersome. He twisted his head shoreward, correcting his course, and saw that the still form in the bow was looking at him.

"Bless us!" he said, shipping the oars and making his way forward to crouch beside her. The woman's gaze was like an unrepentant but redeeming sea dawn after storm. There was nothing to say. She did not stare in fear, needing assurance, or glance in confusion, needing explanation. So Duncan Ross said what Gaels ever said in courteous greeting: "*Fàilte dhuibd; sìth gun robh so.*"

Beaching the boat at Port Erradale, Duncan carried his enigmatic sea gift to the cottage and laid her on the box bed, where he replaced oilskins with blankets. Annie warmed stones to wrap and place at the woman's feet and sides, also heating tea she spooned between lips blue as those of a stillborn baby.

"Give her whisky," Duncan said, and Annie did that as well. Teeth chittered on the spoon by the third dose, as the woman's body suddenly strove for equilibrium in the grounded world.

No marks of injury marred her, but she would not—or could not—speak. Senses were intact, but she made no sound, no reply to gentle questioning in either Gaelic or English.

"Maybe someone knows her," Annie said. "I'll ask about."

Duncan forked his hand through his thick hair, gazing at the woman, again bemused. He looked at Annie: patient, capable—earthly—and shrugged. "Maybe she was visiting someone in Badachro." He hooked his jacket from the floor; the necessary business of fishing.

Annie shawled herself, setting off to make inquiries, leaving Margaret perched on the hearth stool, alternately staring at the now-sleeping figure and re-enacting the seawoman's rescue with her rag doll.

"Give her broth should she wake," Annie instructed before leaving.

It was David's entrance that woke the woman. He came, slanting his *tarsgair* against the cottage wall, splashing clean his hands and arms in a bucket outside the door before entering. "What's this?" he asked, taken aback. The woman's eyes opened, seeing as though through darkness in which she could not be seen.

"She's a selkie Father took from the sea," said Margaret matter-of-factly, having the good Celtic memory for explanatory tales.

"Hmph," said David, skittishly backing from the bed. "Come now, Maggie," he cajoled uneasily in the woman's silence and following gaze. "Who is she really?"

"I told you," said Margaret. "An enchantment stole her voice. I think Father's hidden her pelt somewhere. She belongs with us now."

"She's witless?" whispered David.

"Oh, no," Margaret said, placid in knowledge. "She just can't speak." She hopped up from the stool, stretching to reach the good china bowl from the dresser. David stood, transfixed, uncertain, but Margaret ladled savory fish broth into the bowl and carried it to the bed. "Help her sit up," she commanded.

But the woman shook her head, an abrupt movement startling both David and his sister. The woman sat herself up and took the bowl from Margaret, raising it to her nostrils a moment before handing Margaret the horn spoon and drinking in measured sips directly from the bowl.

Something about her was hypnotic, whether it was the aliveness of her complete silence, the way her hair flowed in profligate waves to pool among the bedcovers, or the drowning color of her eyes. She wore only a shift of Annie's, and David found himself alarmingly aroused. The woman glanced at him suddenly, discerningly, lowering the soup bowl. David quickly turned to the hearth, fumbling at the kettle hanging over the fire, tripping on the stool. He abandoned the endeavor—wanting to curse—snatched a bannock, and fled the cottage.

No one knew her, though the minister spread inquiries parish-wide and beyond. Numerous visitors happened by the Ross cottage in following weeks, on one innocent errand or another, intense curiosity correctly camouflaged. Speculation was lively, avidly suggestive of the sinister. Where Calvinism and paganism met in the Gaelic soul was a realm encompassing unexpected integrations and ingenious permutations comprehensible only to others of the race.

When Duncan first called the woman Rona, a word meaning seal, it was one of the rare times anyone saw her smile, though the smile held not pleasure but irony, a moment of intimacy when distance was all that could be grasped. It was David who was most disturbed by the woman's silence. He interpreted it as too knowing and safely aloof, a position he bitterly coveted. The petty cruelties he inflicted on Rona were punishments he could deny were advertent. Rona seemed untroubled; it was Margaret who noticed and was pained by them, because she loved her brother and the magic she believed was in the sea-woman's wordless presence.

Rona never again slept in the cottage. Instead, she inhabited a bothy on the township's common grazing. It was a dark, dirt-floored hut. Under Rona's care it was always clean, its meager borrowed accoutrements maintained with unrevealing tidiness, as though no one really lived there. Duncan and Annie provisioned her, and, in return, Rona worked the croft with Annie—timely help, as spring planting and peat digging joined survival's other demands.

"I'll be checking out tomorrow," Trinity told Susan, the hostel manager.

"I'll miss you," said Susan. "Where are you off to, then?"

"Gairloch, I suppose. My ancestors went there after the Strathcarron clearances. I'd like to get a look at the place. Is there a hostel there?"

"Three, actually. I think you'd like the lighthouse best, as you're so keen on remote places."

Trinity nodded, already remote. She left the hostel on a last walk, following the familiar lane between sheep parks, drawing up the hood of her jacket as spattering rain arrived on gusts of wind off the firth. Her shoes were soon soaked; she bent her head to shield her face, staring at the ground as she walked, the near instead of the far. Another Ross leaving Ardgay. Trinity stooped to touch the pale silk of a primrose, trying not to feel maudlin, raindrops trickling from petal to finger. Highland weather suited the extremes of lament and glory. But when there was peace it nested with utmost savor, folding restless wings, gestating contentment with life itself rather than with the fruits of ambition.

Trinity turned back to the hostel. Connell stood at the gate. She did not quicken pace; he would wait. When she reached him she stopped, silent. Rain beaded and dripped from the brim of his cap. Under its eave, the jostling gaze.

"Come to Glasgow," he said, hands deep in coat pockets, volatile as a stag glimpsing the spear. "Then, later, come to Ireland. I want you to come. Please. All right?"

"Connell, whatever you're up to.... I can't be party to violence. I can't...."

"No violence," he said.

Rona planted potatoes. The boggy, marginal soil was built up in *feannagan*, the misnomered "lazybeds," using seaweed, bracken, and old thatch piled in strips the previous July, soil heaped on top—soil and decayed vegetation mixed before spring planting. The abundant bracken was used for cattle bedding and mattress stuffing as well.

David plowed the Ross beds, adding manure cleaned from the shielings, using the *cas-chrom* foot plow so disparaged by Lowlanders. It irked David to be old-fashioned, though the work itself brought satisfaction, tranquilizing his mind with the same rhythms to which his forefathers had calmly moved.

Annie and Rona dibbed holes in each bed, pressing seed potatoes into the chill spring ground. Margaret followed to cover the potatoes, fondly patting the soil in time to repetitious child chants. North Erradale, where the Ross family lived, was a sizable crofting township; the women worked in easy hailing distance from other women. The men, this time of year, were out after whitefish. The rocky cove of Port Erradale, just below the crofts, was empty of boats during the lengthening hours of daylight.

Annie didn't mind having to tend crops and livestock in addition to her usual chores, though it taxed energy and efficiency to the utmost. When she thought of former Greenyards neighbors now literally scrambling for a living on shoreland so precipitous they had to tether children and livestock to keep them from falling in the sea, she was grateful for what she had. Others of those neighbors—her best friend, Catherine, for one—had disappeared over the sea on immigrant ships or simply disappeared. After Greenyards, Annie never again felt herself. So profound was this displacement that all succeeding generations were numbed by it. Silence was all her emptied womb—like the emptied glens—now birthed.

Annie feared for Duncan as wives of fishermen always fear: knowing they have nothing with which to bargain for their men's safety in the ocean's fickle precinct. The men sailed out to pilfer the sea's bounty like unrepentant pickpockets with no other choice, staunch in courage and skill. The fishermen made their small propitiations—always turning boats sun-wise on the way out, abiding by a multitude of taboos and superstitions aggravating their ministers.

The word minister, in fact, was never spoken at sea, nor were the words priest, salmon, pig, hare, or rabbit (referred to, if necessary, as little feeties). Annie recalled Hugh MacLean's ordeal the previous winter when trying to bring his boat home in severe weather. He'd held the tiller for fourteen hours on the mountainous, rolling waters of the Minch before risking the shore's murderous beakers. Hugh's grandfather, father, brother, and brother-in-law had all died at sea. Land-loving men. If lucky, their bodies, at least, would be recovered and given the peace of the steady earth. If not, they were food for crabs.

Few men could swim; they reckoned it only prolonged the inevitable. The sea was their sustenance but not their nurturer; their moody goddess but not their friend. They pilfered but did not presume. And the women kept their distance from what was beyond the detritus of the shore—the negligent gifts of wave and tide—not wanting to incite the sea's jealousy. These things were understood, no need to speak of them even inwardly.

Annie bent over the potato bed, glancing sidelong at the woman working quietly beside her. Duncan had gone fishing and returned with this. How could Annie complain? Rona more than earned what little she consumed of their resources. She foraged from the seashore and coaxed a dooryard garden—vegetables instead of the hemp grown for flax by fishermen's wives. Rona was far more asset than dependent, and made no demands, but Annie feared the sea-woman little less than she feared the sea itself.

Rona straightened, gazing over the moors to the shore, and beyond to the bay's scintillating invitation. She felt each glance from Annie, as she felt David's cruelties and his sister's diligent belief. Rona's presence was like a withdrawing tide, inexorable, impersonal, stranding what has been submerged, enticing away what cannot help but dream.

Duncan's catch was mediocre that day, and David's mood sullen. The youth had no affinity for boats and the labyrinth masses of lines and nets requiring iron patience and silken dexterity to handle without calamitous tangling. In his rejecting state of mind, David learned grudgingly, contrary to his own capacities—thinking that he resisted his father and his father's obsolete Gaelic ways when it was really his own instinct for grace he fought. But the sight of scrabbling lobsters made David queasy, and he lacked the will-hardened endurance and sea-tempered acceptance a fisherman's life demanded.

David longed for a distinguished destiny in which he could sever himself from the image of his pregnant mother clubbed by a grinning constable, his father chained in a prison yard. Dread stalked him, whispering in his sleep, sneering over his shoulder at line-bloodied, oar-blistered hands, jeering, "You'll never escape." He'd once heard a schoolmate repeat the words of a 1560 Lowland poem about the Gaels: How *the first Helandman of God was made of An horse turd in Argylle, as is said.* David's people—shite. Anger's corrosion ate through sensitive self-respect into the deeper tissue of identity and the core of David's freedom to create himself.

The Rosses finished their evening meal of potatoes and milk. Rona came down from the bothy to help Annie bait the longline for the next day's cod fishing. Each hook dangled from a horsehair snood attached to the line; Duncan's line had 500 hooks. The work was smelly and unpleasant, using limpets and mussels for bait; and the rain that evening necessitated they do the chore indoors. Rona had gathered the bait that lay piled in baskets beside the long bench.

"Why don't you go shares on one of the bigger boats?" David asked his father. "Won't Roddy MacBain be needing a fourth man when Andrew goes to Canada?"

Duncan was plaiting a horsehair rope, hands deft, face relaxed in the relief of another day's return to solid ground. Though he never flinched from the need to fish, Duncan privately missed the warm-blooded smell of pony and cattle on his hands, and the reliable feel of stone and soil. He didn't look up from his task but said, "Roddy has another cousin in line for that share; no one's looking for a partner just now."

David stood, agitated, but the cottage was too crowded for pacing. He toed a wool basket by the hearth stool, raising his eyes to the women's swiftly moving hands as they baited the hooks, meticulously looping finished sections of the 400-foot line in a large, flat basket.

"We've talked of this before," said Duncan. "I know you don't want to stay on and fish. I need you this spring and summer. After that...." He sighed without meaning to. "After that, you do as you will." He coiled the rope and set it on the bench beside him, rose, and went outside.

Clean wind cut through Duncan's linen shirt—April's fresh breath finding him in the darkness. For a few moments it drove the tight thoughts from his mind, allowing him to simply be a man standing by a stone cottage, strong-bodied and tired. The scatter of neighboring cottages made opaque loaf-shapes between him and the soft, hissing murmur of the bay. The cottage door opened and Rona slid past into the darkness before Duncan could bid her good night.

Dawn was blustery, more rain imminent. March's austere easterly wind had clocked to the prevailing southwest blow that brought Gairloch's chronically rainy weather. Duncan was loading gear into the boat, David tardily joining him, when Rona appeared on the beach. As always she was clothed in the dress and shawl Annie had found for her, but she never looked as other women did. For one thing, her round breasts, mermaid-like, were neither pushed by a corset's agenda nor pulled by gravity's. Rona moved in mesmerizing patterns like a priestess invoking elemental allies. Her movements were a language, intricate but never wasteful, obtuse only if one strained to understand them.

The russet hair was not worn in the matron's manner, covered by an old-fashioned mutch, or styled with maidenly ribbon or fancy Lowland bonnet. It was braided halfway down her back, a cord keeping it from loosening, and from there swung free as if in the process of unbinding itself. She stood barefoot on the beach cobbles and made a series of gestures to Duncan indicating that David should go back to the croft, and she would fish with Duncan.

David was stunned, then flashed an eager look at his father. The offer dumbfounded; women didn't fish—never entered the boats. It was considered unlucky to have a female onboard; red-haired females were unlucky to even encounter on shore preliminary to fishing. Duncan stared at Rona, feeling the layered dimensions of what she communicated, feeling his son's silent pleading and silent scorn, and his own tangled emotions. Fishermen cannot afford tangles; they happen when skill or attention falters, and cause loss, sometimes disaster.

Rona glided to where David stood holding the food Annie had wrapped for midday, and gently tugged it from his hand. She tugged at the front of his coat also, pointing to it, then to herself. David looked at his father. Duncan nodded—once, almost imperceptibly—and David unbuttoned and slid out of the coat, holding it for Rona to don. She drew her shawl over her head, crossing the ends under her chin, wrapping them around her neck and tying them. She kilted her skirts, stepping past Duncan to stow the food packet, then helped the two men heave the boat into the outgoing tide.

Waves scudded whitecapped under a biting wind. Away from shore, Duncan raised the boat's single, loose-footed sail, and shifted from oars to tiller. He steered the boat into Gairloch's bay, skirting the nob of Rubha Bàn and Longa Island's flank, heading at a diagonal across the ocean chop. Rona sat in the bow, hands tucked into the sleeves of David's coat, tendrils of hair fingered loose by the wind, escaping the shawl. Her eyes were grey as the sea in the dawn's thin light.

She seemed content to Duncan, as he was content on the hill with cattle grazing and primroses blooming by the burn. Her contentment soothed him as he had not been soothed since the old days at Greenyards. Her silence wasn't the sullenness he endured from David or the aching stillness of his wife as they lay side-by-side at night. Rona's silence was eternal as sea and mountains, and, if she was troubled, it did not put her at odds with deeper calmness. Despite the stormy day, over the boat abided a climate of peace.

Duncan thought to fish the waters above Badachro, and adjusted the boat's line of travel slightly, taking them toward the fishing stations on Dry Island and Eilean Horisdale, visible in the distance. Rona rapped her knuckles on the gunnel and emphatically shook her head, pointing in a direction nearer the mouth of the bay. Duncan complied without thinking, drawing the tiller toward him to correct their course, tightening the angle of sail.

"You know where the fish are?" he asked, as the boat breasted the chop.

She looked at him, then back in steady concentration on the sea ahead. After a time she gestured to port, and Duncan adjusted course. Ten minutes later, she raised her palm in a sharp, cutting gesture, and Duncan heeled the boat, dropping the sail. Rona moved amidships, taking up the oars to maintain the boat's position against the persuasion of wind and waves and tide. Duncan fastened the end of his longline to a float, dropping the float's anchor overboard, playing out the baited line, intent on smooth effort.

No other boats were close by, but the bay was dotted with craft—mostly four-man operations; a few boats haunted the Minch horizon. There was a bondedness despite distances between boats, as fish are bonded to fishermen despite distancing strata.

That night, Duncan returned to harbor with a felicitous catch of cod. From then on, Rona accompanied him in the boat, while David worked the croft with Annie. This arrangement did not sit well with the community. The Ross family had yet to become locally integrated enough to carry it off without damage to relationships. The township was offended.

Rona already was a continuing topic of gossip; since nothing about her could be verified or clarified, her mystery was inexhaustible. But her maritime partnership with Duncan was bald affront, especially in view of the shining cascades of fish spilling from his wee craft every day.

Sympathy had provided the Rosses a starting place in the process of community assimilation, and Duncan was the kind of man who evoked respect and liking. Annie, too, made favorable impression, though in a less easy-mannered way. But Rona was wordless, kinless, and unruled in a social milieu where word, kin, and rule were paramount. People might forgive Duncan the luck and folly of having Rona, but they would not forgive Rona herself.

The minister called on Duncan. He was Hector Lawrie, shepherd of the flock whose Free Church was south of Strath, in Achtercairn. Until recent times, he had conducted services in a cave; his parishioners considered Reverend Lawrie staunch if joyless. He spoke to Duncan privately, Annie serving precious tea and absenting herself with chores.

"You saved her life and support her admirably," Lawrie said after preliminary pleasantries. "A credit to Christian charitableness."

"It is we who are indebted to her," said Duncan, taking out pipe and tobacco.

The minister forged on. "Ah, well, generous words, and perhaps she's indeed been of help around the place. All the more reason to guide her to seemly prospects of her own. I am thinking of Alie Fraser over in Strath, a widower of good habits, and a fine cobbler. I know he would welcome a quiet wife."

Duncan drew on his pipe, repulsed by the image of Alie Fraser's stringy hands prodding Rona's soul. He took the pipe from his mouth. "I think she can find a husband on her own if she's minded to. Rona's far from lack-wit, you know," he said mildly.

Reverend Lawrie set down his teacup with a sharp click. "You exploit her—or else encourage dangerous whims. Either way you err, having her in that boat. She needs husband and home to settle her, prevent such as her from wantonness."

Duncan said nothing for a few minutes. He leaned forward and knocked the dottle from his pipe onto the hearthstone. "She is nae wanton."

"Maybe we should help Rona find a husband." Annie's voice came unexpectedly in the darkness where she and

Duncan lay in bed a week after Reverend Lawrie's visit. "I've noticed many unmarried men look her way."

"Unmarried and married," Duncan amended. He grieved that Annie was afraid—grieved that he had not made her happy as she had been in the old days at Greenyards: that instead, he had exacerbated her unhappiness. "She's a woman grown, and capable of making her own match if she desires one," he said. "Is her presence so unbearable to you?"

Duncan felt his wife's stiffness without touching her. My Annie, he thought, pain fresh in him.

"Margaret ever follows her—as do David's eyes. She leads you to the fish, and our neighbors gossip and shake their heads, envying and pitying. She is making us separate."

"She is helping us prosper."

"Aye. And how does she know what she knows?"

Duncan walked beside his wife's cousin, James MacBeath, on the way back from kirk that Sunday. Annie, as always, stayed home with Margaret, and David trailed behind the men, strolling with Angus and Donnie MacBeath. Annie's kin lived mostly in Big Sand, between North Erradale and Strath. Rona never attended church. It was rumored she had made a pact with the devil, bartering her voice for the ability to silently summon fish—and men as well. The rumors spawned variations, shoals of elusive, darkly glimmering perhapses.

James MacBeath was not a busybody but felt the concerns and responsibilities of kinship. The subject of Rona made him acutely uncomfortable. Duncan was someone James admired—and was junior to in years. He cleared his throat, signaling an impending shift in the conversation that had thus far touched on weather, bulls, and the laird's new cruck-framed threshing barn over in Flowerdale.

"Brought in a bright fish or two this past month, haven't you?" James observed.

"Aye, a few," said Duncan.

"That Rona has been some useful around the boat, I hear."

"Aye, she has."

They proceeded a ways, smoking their pipes, hands in trousers pockets.

"Talked with Iain Dubh a week past," James said, eyes habitually scanning the bay's horizon as they walked. "He's looking for a wife now he's come into his own place there in Strath. Iain is young still, but steady."

Duncan said nothing.

"In the long run of things, reputation's all a man can hold, as you no doubt know. You're a strong man, Duncan, but there's Annie...."

"David'll be gone by autumn. Annie will only have wee Margaret to help on the croft, and I'll have no one for the boat. What sense is in it, James, bidding Rona away?"

James trudged alongside Duncan, and the two men puffed on their pipes. Behind them, the youths conferred in low tones about well-paying opportunities in the south.

Ostensibly, no one worked on the Sabbath. No one made merry, either. The church scowled on dancing, fiddle playing, and fun in general—and especially on Sundays, such things must be shunned. There were Sabbath services in Gaelic at noon and in English at two, and usually a six-o'clock meeting as well. At home were Bible readings, prayers, psalms.

Rona gathered bait on Sunday, heedless of religious dictates. She walked backward along the edge of the sea, carrying a small spud and a fishing basket. The best time of day to catch razor-shells—or spout-fish as they were properly called—was between noon and two during ebb tides in spring. Rona backed slowly, her bare feet tough but cognizant of variations of terrain. A razor-fish impetuously spouted from the wet beach, and Rona's spud instantly slanted into the sand inches from the spout hole, pushing until encountering obstruction. She crouched, carefully removing sand until the shell was uncovered. Care was essential—the top of the razor-fish drew blood if touched.

Rona scooped sand away from the fish's sides until she could grip the shell with thumb and forefinger, pulling gently so that shell not detach from fish. Razor-fish were the best of bait, and, cleaned, made fine soup stock as well.

Rona basketed the fish and stood, about to move on. From the hillside a burn flowed off the moor, furrowing through peat, cutting a path down the steep slope to the beach, spreading its eager course over sand and cobbles to reach the sea. Where the burn's fresh water mingled with salt ocean, Rona saw a seal's head surface. Woman and seal glimpsed each other at the same moment, a glimpse prolonged in communion, wordless and therefore timeless in the discourse of being, as waves hissed upon the shore, drowning the need for any other voice.

There were more appealing sections of Glasgow than the one to which Connell directed Trinity as they entered Scotland's most rambunctious city. Connell led her to a flat, rank and compressed, where he dropped his duffle on the floor and plugged in the ubiquitous kettle. Trinity lowered her suitcase beside the bed and dubiously surveyed the two-room habitation Connell had described as belonging to a friend. "A wee love nest," she murmured.

Connell shot her a warning look.

Trinity shrugged. "Ply me with tea and seduce me," she suggested. "Maybe it'll look better horizontally."

Connell shook his head, turning to the cupboard for mugs. "Bloody American princess," he muttered, his back to her.

Trinity crossed the four steps from bedroom to kitchen and carefully slid her arms around his waist, his back still toward her. She'd learned not to startle him. "Is your flat in Belfast like this?"

"Little better," he said.
"Not very romantic," observed Trinity.
"You'd rather be fucking out on the moor?"
Trinity unbuckled his belt. "Let's give this a try."

Connell went out alone the next day. Trinity wandered the neighborhood streets but was not refreshed by her walk. Nerves contracted from sensory overload and the unlovely nuances of her situation—unsubtle as the tenement's smell. It was not a place for tenderness.

"You're here with a woman? You must be joking," the Armagh man facing Connell across the pub table leaned back as if Connell carried contagion.

Connell drew on his cigarette, flicked ash onto the floor. "She's a harmless American tourist with the usual hired car. She doesn't ask questions; she's cover, not threat."

Rory sneered. "I know what she covers." He slowly leaned forward, displaying meaty arms on the tabletop. "You listen. Too much is at stake. Get shot of her."

Trinity was asleep, far retreated into an interior Highlands, when Connell came in. She had left the kitchen light on for him; Connell paused in the bedroom doorway, looking at the slender figure on the bed. Trinity lay half-covered by the sleeping bag, slim hands folded on her belly. The oversized T-shirt she wore made her seem like a young girl, but it was the sheltering pose of the hands that moved Connell. He took a step forward, drawn by what is fragile yet steadfast, but stopped before reaching the bed, excluded by boundaries whose origins Connell no longer could identify.

He soundlessly backed, turning, padding to the kitchen cupboard for glass and whisky bottle. At the door's betraying creak, he heard the sleeping bag's rustle and Trinity's voice saying his name as though she wakened on the long, green crest of a wave.

On an afternoon in late May, when barley planting was finished, and it was too early yet to bring the Ross cows to their shieling bothy for milking, David thought about poaching a salmon from the river. The day was mild and hazy. Salmon poaching, like rabbit snaring—also forbidden—was nothing like sea fishing. It didn't involve boats or lines or grinding hours of perilous effort. Sneakily gaffing a salmon was an exercise in guile: to catch the elusive fish and elude being caught by the gamekeeper.

David was considering which river pool to investigate when he saw a towering, well-bearded man in a kilt approaching the Ross cottage. Except on occasions such as weddings, the sight of a kilted man was uncommon. This man's bearing and strong good looks sparked embers of David's buried cultural pride. He courteously greeted the visitor, who looked to be about twenty-five though carried the dignity of an elder, and asked what brought him to North Erradale.

"I'm told this is where to find the cottage of Duncan Ross," the man answered.

"Aye, you've found it. I'm David Ross."

"Duncan MacKenzie from Kinlochewe. I'm told there is a woman called Rona here; I was hoping to speak to her."

"Duncan MacKenzie, the bard?" Even David still respected bards; MacKenzie was well known for his satires and songs. Though himself not a good singer, he had established his bardic reputation at an astonishingly young age.

"Aye, that's myself," he said, "though it's as a weaver I make my way." MacKenzie had received no formal schooling. He lived as a crofter, his natural gifts articulating themselves in weavings both material and oral, dyed in the land's clear hues.

"Rona is with my father in the boat. My mother will have tea for you if you want to wait. You know Rona doesn't speak."

"I've heard that," said the bard. "All the same, she tells a story."

MacKenzie was contemplatively seated on the bench outside her bothy when Rona came home from the day's fishing. The evening's blue light, blurring what was distant, brought lucidity to what was near, and when Rona came toward him the bard saw her as the land's only reality. She slipped past him, ducking her head to enter the bothy, emerging a while after with two bowls of porridge, handing him one and seating herself on a stone nearby.

MacKenzie observed her calm fatigue. There was an unbreakableness about her, as though nothing was left to shatter. Suffering sank like a stone through endless depths of shifting, translucent color. Her edges were as definite and transitory as the rim of a wave.

The bard ate his porridge, occasionally waving midges away from his face and obliquely studying the sea-woman. He set aside his bowl when he saw her do so, and lit his pipe. Clouds of smoke kept insects at bay as dusk imperceptibly drained light from the day's surface.

"My brother is a piper," MacKenzie said after introducing himself, looking away from Rona into the silky distance. "He received his gift of music from the fairies at Sitheanan Dubha, an isle in Loch Maree. So he tells me, and whether I believe it or not does not matter."

MacKenzie puffed on his pipe, his long, well-shaped legs comfortably crossed, his back against the rough stone of Rona's bothy. The bard's keen gaze drifted slowly down from the moors, resting with a warmth like summer afternoon on the motionless figure in front of him. He spoke kindly. "There was a mermaid Roddy MacKenzie caught when he was a young man in Port Henderson. He let her go on the promise that no person ever drown from one of his boats, and none have; his boats are famous to this day. I hear that Duncan Ross pulled you from the sea, but you have made him no promises."

The bard paused. "I stay in Kinlochewe," he said, "with tunes that can fill a silence, and silence to keep it company, and tales when explanations seem needed." He regarded her a few moments more, then stood, tucking away his pipe. "Thank you for the food. Kinlochewe is said to be a pretty place, though not by the sea. I would let no one harm you." He smiled slightly. "Satire is edged as any blade." He walked past her down the path, an easy grace in his long stride, the swing of the kilt.

The ocean heaved as if trying to throw off aggravation, rolling shrugs warning of prolonged storm farther out. Duncan was at the oars, maneuvering among offshore rocks as Rona retrieved lobster creels. It was tricky work even in sheltered inlets. Their weeks of partnership in the boat had yielded the kind of almost telepathic teamwork David had refused to develop with his father. Duncan still wished he could farm the land instead of fish, but the hours in the boat with Rona were balm to his spirit, regardless of weather.

Most of the time Duncan simply accepted this, with much the same cast of mind that had enabled him to accept his term in prison. He didn't wrestle with issues of what was or was not deserved. His thoughts intuitively engaged with integrity's principles, leaving matters of outcome to larger, less explicable forces. David, by opposing his father, claimed only the arena in which action is considered on the basis of reaction, with all its dilemmas and excruciating self interest.

Duncan was not unaware of Rona's effect on him—or of how she affected his son—but he neither struggled against it nor abandoned the sense of propriety that, although differing from community expectation, guided him. Rona, who seemed a law unto herself, nonetheless had fragile immunity and unknown recourse. Whatever sanctuary Duncan and Rona offered one another dwelled amid perilous realms.

Rona hauled a creel from the water, lifting it over the gunnel. Inside, two monster-looking lobsters clacked in a tangle of legs, carapaces, and waving pincers. Duncan backed the boat into a shoving wave. His oar scraped rock and caught in a crevice. The boat banged an elbow of stone, jolting Rona. She flung out an arm to brace herself. Her hand slipped, and she slammed against the edge of the gunnel, barely preventing herself from tumbling overboard.

Duncan, freeing the trapped oar, wheeled the boat, pulling strongly to clear the rocks. Rona untangled herself from the gear and sat with an arm pressed against her side.

"Is it bad?" Duncan asked, when their position sufficiently improved.

Rona shook her head.

They came ashore an hour later.

"Go up to the house. Annie will make you a compress," Duncan said. "I can unload alone."

But when he got to the cottage Rona was not there, and Annie had not seen her.

"She well may have cracked ribs," he told his wife.

"She is not wanting aid from me," Annie replied. "You and Margaret are the only ones she lets near." Annie folded her arms over her midriff, watching Duncan clump around the cottage in his wellies, gathering flannel strips and salve, face still ruddy from sea wind. "Take Margaret to help you."

Duncan looked up from his preoccupation. "It's not needing more than two hands," he said.

His wife made no reply. Duncan saw how she clenched herself, sleeves rolled up on chapped arms no more weathered and work worn than Rona's, but lacking the sea-woman's cunningly boned elegance. "I'll take her for the cheer she'll bring," he said.

But Margaret's play had drawn her out of hailing range. Duncan climbed the path to Rona's bothy and rapped his knuckles on the door lintel before pulling aside the hide covering that served as a door, crossing the low threshold into the darkness within. He stood a moment, vision adjusting, feeling an inner turbulence alien to his expectations of himself.

Rona was not there. Duncan laid the medical supplies on the hearth and walked back outside. He stood with hands on hips, scanning pastures and moors before striding down the path to the sea.

She was floating naked in the water at the third cove he tried. His gaze was arrested, as it had first been in the April dawn of finding her. But this time the woman knew his presence, righting herself in waist-deep water as Duncan made his way across the cobbles. The purple bruising on her ribs was sullen against pale skin. Her hair, darkened by water, clung in long parentheses over shoulders, breasts, hips.

At the edge of the water Duncan stopped, waves sliding in to eddy at his boots. "Maybe you are safer in the water than atop it," he said to the woman standing half-exposed to the spring air, half-committed to the judgment of the known.

Rona moved forward, coming into shallow water, emerging from the sea as though created within movement's revelation. Duncan's lips parted, breath catching in the sudden constriction that shunts all awareness to eyes and groin. His hand involuntarily lifted.

Rona halted as though it warded instead of reached for her. She backed, sinking into covering waters until only her face was seen, and Duncan turned, trudging home.

Trinity woke to find Connell sleeping beside her, the second time in all the weeks of lovemaking that they actually had spent a night together in a bed. Connell occupied the space beside her differently than had her husband, who slumbered as though artfully arranged for viewing in a casket. Connell looked felled instead of arranged.

Rumbling morning traffic trembled the tenement. Dawn had a certain smell here; Trinity noted its rise joining the night smell of the mattress. Strange to find herself with man and mattress and the shake of urban industry. She curled against Connell's back, reaching around to caress. Connell groaned, pressing Trinity's hand into a tighter grip, then rolled onto his back. He pulled Trinity atop him, only half-awake. Climax came quickly; Connell relaxed his bruising hold, murmuring an apology.

"You'd think it was the first time in months—or the last," she said.

He abruptly rose, reaching for clothes he'd dropped on the floor the night before. "You'll need to be out of here by this afternoon," he told her as he zipped his jeans and jerked a T-shirt over his head, then unfastened the jeans to tuck the shirt in.

Trinity watched with incomplete detachment. Connell looked at her. "I'll call you in Gairloch. The lighthouse, right? We'll make plans then."

She waited until Connell was in the kitchen, brewing tea and rolling a cigarette, before pushing aside the sleeping bag and methodically dressing. She went barefoot into the kitchen and sat on a stool at the Formica counter that served as a table.

Connell slide a cup of tea in front of her, but Trinity felt nauseous, as she did most mornings now, and shook her head. "Not this morning, thanks," she said.

"Toast?"

"Sure."

Connell put two slices of bread into the toaster and stood staring at the appliance as though it operated solely on human concentration.

"Can we go to a park or something? Go for a walk?" Trinity asked into the ludicrous silence.

"A park?"

The toaster popped, making them both flinch. Connell flipped the toast onto a plate and rummaged in a drawer for a knife. He snapped shut the drawer and began buttering the toast. Trinity had never seen him so nervous. It was oddly undisturbing in the moment's domesticity, however illusory the ordinariness.

Connell set the plate of toast in front of Trinity, removing the offending cup of tea.

"Thank you," she said.

Connell put two more slices into the toaster, shoving the lever down, and faced Trinity. "You're thinking I won't call you, that I'll just disappear."

She gently pushed the plate toward Connell. "You eat these. I don't want butter on mine."

"Aren't you feeling well?" he asked, diverted, looking hard at her. "Trin…Christ, are you…?"

"I'm fine," she said hurriedly. "I'm just upset. It's wrenching, whether or not you call."

"I'll call!"

A sly rap at the door cut into their privacy. Connell looked at Trinity. "Stay inside," he said, cracking open the door, then unhooking the chain and slipping out into the hall, closing the door behind him.

"What's gone wrong?" Connell asked.

Rory lit a cigarette and leaned against the stained wall of the stairwell. "Nothing's wrong. I've been thinking about what you said, about your girlfriend with her innocuous hired car and her innocuous American face. I'm thinking we'd do well to have such a car and such a driver to take us to Stranraer and across."

"No."

Rory shifted his pose, straightening from the wall and dropping his cigarette, grinding it into the wood floor with the heavy toe of his black work shoe. "Once it hits the news she'll know what you've done—unless she's totally witless. Better she's implicated enough to keep her trap shut."

"No. We'll carry through as planned."

The two faced each other in the dim hall, the condensed shadows.

"Either she comes, or her mouth must be stopped," Rory said. "It's your own doing."

"No," he said a third time, the Celtic rhythm of verity. "The risk is only to me. She's never seen you or heard your name."

Both men knew that Rory was armed, and Connell was not. Tension stretched until it was simply suffering, a familiarity as close to the soul as beauty.

"Then we leave now," Rory hissed. "Damn you for a dick-headed fool."

Trinity was no longer in the kitchen when Connell returned. She sat on the edge of the bed, folding clothes into her suitcase.

Connell stood in the bedroom doorway. "I have to leave. Now. Don't go outside until I'm well away. Don't look out the window. I'll call you in Gairloch. Don't doubt it. I'll call."

Trinity stared at him, dropped the jumper she was folding, then picked it up and carefully, crookedly, refolded it, laying it into the suitcase as if lowering a baby into a cradle. "You said no violence."

"I lied." Trinity watched him stuff clothes and shaving gear into his duffle. "To get two nights with you in a bed like decent human beings, in this stinking tenement you despise."

"Connell...."

He was heedless. She closed her eyes, heard the zipper close on his bag and the quick sound of his tread. He left without touching her.

David was fixated on the notion that Rona could speak if she chose to. He attempted to startle sounds from her and ignored or pretended not to understand the gestures of communication she offered. David's friends sniggered when discussing the sea-woman. They prodded David for details to excite the libido, capitalizing on David's disrespect, and David suffered, torn between the attention generated by half-invented tales of Rona and ingrained family loyalties.

Annie sat outside the cottage at her spinning wheel while Rona wound spun hanks of wool on the *crois-iarna*, readying the yarn for dyeing. Down on the shore Duncan was repairing creels, sitting with several of the neighboring men.

The morning was soft, pearly sky and green braes, the bay a silver-blue that lightened into a blurred band of white at the horizon. The Isle of Skye was shrouded, the impression of emptiness across the sea making the near world of the croft, and the soft Gaelic voices floating up from the shore, all the more intimate.

"There's to be a ceilidh tonight," Annie said. The spinning wheel steadily whirled; the women never stopped working. Knitting was done while women walked, while they hauled peat and herded beasts. By sticking one needle into the waistband's *sopachan*, a hand was left free for other tasks. Only in sleep did their hands rest.

Annie glanced at Rona. "You should come."

Rona gave a slight shake of the head.

"You ought, for our sakes if not your own."

David appeared in the cottage doorway, feet braced. "You're wasting your time, Mother. She'll never be more than Father's dumb foundling, more mute than a swan."

The spinning wheel stopped. "You'll apologize," Annie said, "to us both."

David's face pinched. He pushed away from the door and strode past them. "Sorry, Mother...Rona."

Three fiddlers, including Duncan Ross, attended the ceilidh. Ewan Fraser brought his pipes, and old Donald MacLean his speedy pennywhistle. The dancing, debating, and storytelling were tireless. The people's bond with music was unseverable. If religion was their sinew and kinship their marrow, music was their blood—vital, bright, quick-flirting as a burn.

Several fine singers attended as well: Murdina and Ishbel MacBeath, and Angus MacKenzie. The evening overspilled spring's cupped palm. The calls of thrush and cuckoo sweetened the intervals. Swallows swooped around cottage eaves, lambs bleated. Along the beach, gulls congregated on cobbles and boat gunnels. The township's young men similarly congregated, and the young women flocked. Older folks observed them, missing nothing, and children infiltrated as they ever do.

Annie tried to afford Rona the advantage of her company, but the sea-woman faded sideways under the pressure of socializing. Margaret periodically abandoned her peers to lean at Rona's side, fingers twined with those of the sea-woman. Something twisted in Annie at the sight of this, as if seeing her daughter enmeshed in a drowning filigree of kelp.

Duncan played the fiddle, and he also danced, setting aside his instrument to cut tricky steps with Annie's nimble Aunt Effie or Effie's formidable older sister Kirsty. Annie herself could no longer be coaxed into even the rarest waltz; after Greenyards she no longer danced, and it was a loss, because the sight of Annie and Duncan dancing would make even the most dour cynic smile.

The men spent longer and longer intervals clustered outside, drinking. The joking got rougher; some of the older folk drifted homeward – ceilidhing wasn't like it had been in the past. Whisky thickened the mood but did not slow or blur the music, and the singing was clear and pure as dawn. Children collapsed into abrupt slumbers as the night progressed. Men, young and old, slyly watched Rona, but none extended a hand in invitation, until Donnie Bain's younger brother, Iain, approached, foolish grin on his flushed, hard-boned face.

"Dance?" he asked, grabbing her hand.

She shook her head, a tight, shuddering movement. Iain tugged, the grin broadening and fading in shifting, incomplete cycles of reaction.

"Sure ye want. Let's dance. Come to it, now."

Rona felt the gazes on her, the lack of sympathy, the sweaty hand grasping her like an undertow. She moved forward. The music sprang at her, and Iain pulled Rona into a spinning embrace, clasping her too closely, his hand too low on her waist. He dipped and pranced with a conqueror's vanity, and the township watched.

One fiddle of the three dropped out of the music. A moment later, a persuasive hand intervened, gently and seamlessly, between Iain and his unwilling partner. Duncan's move left Iain in a momentary dwam, bewilderedly swaying for several blinks before he realized he had lost his partner. He lowered his head as if to charge at the dancers but could not collect sufficient focus amid the swirl of couples, so staggered in search of refreshment.

At Duncan's harboring touch, Rona relaxed; Duncan felt her body receive the music, translate it into sensuality's language. For a moment Duncan met and mirrored this, then swung her to the sidelines, releasing her before the music ended. He returned to his fiddle; Rona slipped away while eyes still followed him, gone before anyone but Annie noticed.

Duncan and Jamie lounged on the hill with a fail-dyke at their backs. The land rolled in swelling green humps and waves down to the shore. Rectangles of lusher green marked where *achaidhgan* had enriched the soil. For several weeks cattle were driven into the *achadh* each night after milking, in order to manure those temporary stone- and turf-walled enclosures. The ground was then turned with the cas-chrom and planted with black oats, the walls allowed to topple, and new achaidhgan constructed elsewhere. Soil was poor and drained slopes scarce.

Crofting had only been in existence in Gairloch since 1845. Dr. John MacKenzie, the estate's factor during young laird Osgood's minority, created rent-racked townships of four or five acre (or smaller) crofts. While actual clearances in Gairloch were few, there had been a dismaying loss of common graze, and the factor tried diligently to change how tenants lived. Crofters were commanded to dig drainages, remove stones from fields, and rotate crops, planting rye and clover, cabbages, turnips, and carrots. The growing of barley—used for distilling whisky—was discouraged.

MacKenzie was vexed by the dearth of iron-wheeled carts and offended by tenant cottages with their dung heaps, and their doorways shared by beasts and humans alike. For their part, the crofters were unenthused by Dr. MacKenzie's improvement plans. When the factor resigned, the year Duncan joined the community, tenants returned to old practices.

Duncan gently toyed with an unfurling bracken stem beside him. The two men and their sons had been working on the *garradh fail*, the fail-dyke of stone and turf creating graze boundaries. The men's sons now diminished in the distance, efficiently slouching toward the village of Strath. A strong breeze streamed over the moor from the northwest, the men partially sheltered from it by the dyke behind them.

Jamie leaned an elbow on a cushion of sphagnum. "You heard how Alie Watson down at Big Sand broke his leg in a fall Saturday past?"

"I heard, aye," said Duncan.

"Neill Watson asked if you mightn't be interested in Alie's place in the boat whilst he heals. Six weeks it will be, drift-netting for herring."

Duncan tipped his head back against the dyke, staring at the shouldered bulk of Skye across the water, the slender isle of Rona beside it. "Does the rest of the crew want me as well?"

"Oh, aye," Jamie said. "They're anxious not to fall behind or have to take on an untried lad. Neill's spoken with the others." MacBeath raised himself to a sitting position and took out his tobacco. "A fourth share of herring brings far better than lobsters, now the cod is ended." He held out the tobacco pouch.

"I'll talk to Neill," Duncan said after a pause, accepting the offering.

Rona stacked chunks of peat into the willow creel—the day's final load. Half-ten in the evening, the June sky still alight; by solstice only two shy hours of darkness would divide day from day. With Duncan part of Neill Watson's crew, Rona had returned to landed toil. It eroded her; her spirit slipped away. At every pause Rona looked out to the sea, gaze sorting through the distant fishing boats, sliding beyond them to the Minch's horizon.

She hoisted the full creel onto her back, its strap across her chest, and followed the path away from the peat dig the Rosses had inherited with the MacKenzie croft. The evening gusted with damp, aching wind. She plodded, compressed by weariness. Where the path crossed a stiled dyke, Rona encountered David and two companions. One was Angus MacBeath; the other was blond, beefy Donnie MacLeod, his finger hooked in the handle of a whisky jug. Donnie's father, like many township men, operated an illegal still.

Angus occupied the stile. Usually placating, Angus adopted whatever emotional climate surrounded him. These days Donnie tended to dominate that climate. The MacLeods had once been lords of Gairloch. In 1494 their lands were lost to the MacKenzies by writ of fire and sword. MacLeods who remained in the area never forgot that savage wresting away of clan tenure, though after almost 400 years it was less frequently brought up in conversation. Donnie's inherited resentments neatly aligned with present dissatisfactions.

Rona backed away from the stile, realizing the net awaiting her.

"Rest, have a drink," suggested Donnie, slipping behind her. He brutally jerked the edge of Rona's creel, pulling her off balance. She sat down hard, peat spilling. Before she could free herself of the chest strap, Donnie used it to pin her arms.

"Give her a drink, Angus," he said thickly to the youth who, at seventeen, was four years Donnie's junior. "It's time she learned to be sociable."

Angus, drunk and excited, stumbled off to the stile to pick up the jug Donnie had dropped.

"Hold her," Donnie panted, struggling to keep Rona captive.

David joined them, straddling her legs and sitting on them, immobilizing Rona's head between his hands while Angus attempted to force whisky between her clenched teeth. The harsh liquid spilled down her dress front. "Ach, you've wet her clothes, Angus; best take them off her like a good lad."

Angus' eyes darted fearfully from Donnie to David, making sure the instruction was serious permission.

"Don't worry, you sod," scoffed Donnie. "Come on. Let's get a look at her."

David's eyes were fixed in denial, his breathing ragged.

"You'll have to get the strap out of the way," Angus said, voice high.

The three maneuvered, holding Rona on her back, David still straddling her.

"Take her, Davy," urged Donnie.

David pushed up the skirt and shift. "Hold her legs," he grunted to Angus. "Go on," he hissed into Rona's ear as he shoved himself inside her. "Scream. I know you can. Go on. Go on." He doggedly plunged, terrified, hating everyone, bucking into abrupt orgasm, teeth gritted.

"Someone's on the path!" Donnie said, tight with frustration.

Angus tottered to his feet in panic. "Oh, Jesus."

David rolled from atop Rona, wildly fumbling at his breeks. He stumbled away, following Donnie into the concealing folds of the hills.

When shepherd John Fraser reached the stile and the overturned creel, no one was there.

It was morning before David approached his parents' cottage. Duncan was still out on the water. Inside, Margaret was sweeping the packed dirt floor. Annie came in from tending stock to find her son looking gutted, stinking of self-loathing.

"What's this?" She glanced at Margaret. "Carry these scones to Mrs. MacRae who's ailing," she told her daughter. "Sit with her and see if she needs aught done."

Alone with David she waited, arms folded. David looked at the floor. "Has…has Rona come in?" he asked.

Annie shook her head, hands clenching. "I have not seen her yet today. What have you done, David?"

"I…forced myself on her."

Annie caught her breath. "Alone?"

"'Twas I did it."

Annie's arms dropped to her sides. She turned away from her son, leaning one hand on the dresser, the other resting a moment over her womb; again the truncheon's blow. She drew her shawl over her head and left the cottage.

Rona's bothy was empty. Annie let drop the door curtain and gazed, as her husband once had, over the moors toward the sea.

When Duncan came in from the night's herring fishing, his son was at the shielings with the cattle and sheep and ponies, where he would stay the rest of the summer. Duncan searched for Rona, systematically following the shoreline, cove-by-cove, climbing headlands. He went north, away from beaches where were nets were strung on poles to dry and boats with their sharply sloping stems and sterns canted on brick-red cobbles, waiting for the next evening's venture.

At a cup-like inlet where black ledges of stone reached into cold, swaying water, Duncan found her. The sun was high: June's cherishing lucence. Rona, caught in that light, was illumined like an abalone shell whose body has been pillaged, its inner splendor unwillingly exposed. Duncan's feelings for her surfaced like a dolphin out of strata colored in silence, creation's gestation—its first breath the signal exhale between sky and sea.

At the rattle of cobbles noising Duncan's approach, Rona lifted her gaze to stare at him, and Duncan felt the fear a man knows when cornering something irredeemably wild. Rona was standing at the water's edge, skirt hem darkened and sandy. Her shawl was gone, her mesmerizing hair unbound. One cheek was bruised. Duncan saw marks on her arms, and her lower lip was split and swollen.

She retreated into the shallows as Duncan neared. He halted.

"Don't," he said. "I won't touch you."

She waded deeper, water dragging at her skirt.

"Rona—no." He plunged forward, splashing into the water, but Rona swam now, shrugging out of her clothes, the dress drifting half-submerged like a drowned woman.

Duncan stopped thigh-deep in the water. He could not swim. Rona turned her head, looking at him in speech that could never be misunderstood or explained, then left him.

In late March the following year, when oat planting had begun but before larches had fully greened, Duncan trudged home from cod fishing to find Annie sitting outside the cottage, knitting. Margaret sat nearby, rocking a rosy, grey-eyed baby.

Duncan stared.

"Rona brought him to Mother," Margaret whispered. "Isn't he fine as anything?"

Annie raised her eyes to her husband; the knitting never faltered. "Murdoch," she said. "He is Murdoch Ross."

Trinity rode to Gairloch on buses, from Glasgow through Stirling and Perth to Inverness, where she stayed overnight at a student hostel. It was over breakfast next morning that she heard a voice on the kitchen radio pronounce Connell dead.

She continued her journey, fleeing Inverness as if Connell's death resided in that one room, unreal elsewhere. On the one-lane road past Achnasheen and Kinlochewe, she swayed through curves, mountains filling her view, rock smoothed by sea-like eons. They passed Loch Maree, whose waters people of old found healing.

The bus left her at Strath, and Trinity overnighted in a bed and breakfast, catching the post-bus to Malveig next morning. The road wound past Big Sand and North Erradale, the postie braking more often for sheep than for other vehicles on the thrifty ribbon of road.

At Malveig, the manager of the lighthouse hostel picked her up, the road narrowing still further in the final stretch, the van blithely swooping up and over knolls, cautiously hurrying over what seemed flimsy bridges spanning chasms, but this drama didn't penetrate. It was merely cinematic.

At the lighthouse she deposited her suitcase on a lower bunk, drifted into the cramped kitchen for a mug of tea, and wandered outside where she stood at the white, waist-high wall enclosing the lighthouse. Below was the sea, sparkling inanely blue. Tables of red and black rock slanted into the waves. Forty miles distant floated the Western Isles. Nearer, to the southwest, Skye overshadowed Rona.

Trinity walked—heather and bog, grey stones and prodding wind. At times, the familiarity of Highland terrain was soothing, mindless as breathing. At other moments, her senses were suddenly crazed by it, burned by the not-as-yet cauterizing beauty of landscape.

She walked compulsively, following sheep paths along headlands steeply dropping to a sea of turquoise, indigo, slate, aquamarine, lapis; aventurine where shallows covered white sand. Sea stacks reared, clefts of booming surf. Cormorants and shags skidded on the ocean surface, leaving white trailing wakes in their landings, the skittering flap of wings distinct above the rhythmic hush of waves. Gulls wheeled above and below Trinity as she followed the coastline, climbing higher, walking a wind-pushed edge inside herself.

Next day was the same, only the weather had changed: low, darkly driven clouds and punishing bursts of rain. Trinity went south; more headlands and moors, sea-cliffs less dramatic and beaches less sandy, but still the rock spires, sea-damp caves, wind-penetrated cliffs where the elements consummated terms of balance during millions of years of intercourse.

The Western Isles were invisible; even Skye was shrouded. Long, surging rollers heaved in from the Minch, steel grey, undercast in green, frothing over beach cobbles, smashing and spilling their careless lace over stone. Trinity slogged across saturated moors, abandoning the fussy technique of using hummocks of heath as stepping stones through what seemed continuous bog. Shoes were soaked, clothes sodden. It didn't matter.

The clothes were still damp when she set out the third day, the sky still grey, as though differentiation of any kind would never again occur in Trinity's experience. She walked south again with the vague thought to reach North Erradale. Beyond Malveig, she stopped to rest on a stone that offered a view along the coast. The wind waited; weather fronts negotiated. Midges took advantage of the stillness.

Trinity stood again, goaded to move on, and caught sight of a seal in the cup-like cove below. From her vantage, Trinity could see the seal's entire body through diaphanous water. It was one of the oddly russet-marked grey seals found only in the vicinity of Skye.

Without conscious decision, Trinity began picking her way down the sea-cliff. At first there were tiers of narrow sheep paths, but these petered out where soil became stone, the slope dropping sheer to the beach. Trinity paused, glancing at the seal still skimming in search of fish in the cove. She adjusted her daypack and zipped her windbreaker to keep it from catching on rock, then began the descent.

She faced inward, edging fingers and shoe tips into crumbly crevices, sometimes encountering tiny bouquets of sea-pinks or incandescent moss. Her body shook with strain, but she didn't slip. She dropped the final five feet onto the cobbles, grunting with the jar of pain. Belatedly, she wondered, with her first flash of emotional clarity, how she would get back up.

Scanning the cove for signs of whether a rising tide would entirely engulf the beach, Trinity saw what initial investigation would have revealed: the cove was accessible from the south, where sheep paths threaded a less-precipitous drop. Trinity shrugged off her daypack and stowed the windbreaker. The seal's head popped up from the water fifteen yards away, staring at Trinity. She lowered herself onto a smooth red boulder, gazing back.

For over an hour the seal kept her company, sometimes shooting to and fro under the surface, sometimes lolling in the rocking waves, or vertically bobbing, head above water, contemplating Trinity in what seemed interest, even sympathy. A fine mist of rain descended.

Trinity stiffly rose, donning windbreaker and pack. "Good-bye," she said to the seal. She felt there was more to say but could not begin, so walked across the cobbles to the sheep trail and started climbing.

Rain increased, the footing dangerously slick. Three-quarters of the way up, Trinity angled on a tangent to shelter beneath a rock overhang. She leaned backward against the slope, then dropped her pack and sat, finding a niche between stones, her back against a crevice from which wafted a chill, cave-like draught. Rain hypnotically dripped from the overhang. The sea below was stippled by legions of falling drops, waves subdued under tiny pricks, midges bedeviling a giant.

Trinity dozed. She dreamed a fairy came to her, a man handsome as Connell, and asked if she had seen Fionaghalla.

"No," she said sadly, "I was blindfolded."

She woke when there was a sound like a door slamming deep in the rock behind her, and the cold stream of air abruptly ceased. She shuddered, disoriented, pushing to her feet to continue the climb. Suddenly, she realized she had left her hat on the beach where she had used it to cushion her seat on the stone.

Automatically, she started back down the slope, retracing her route. The rain had stopped; clouds were thinning and parting, sun breaking through. The seal was gone.

As Trinity hurried down the final stretch of scree, she fell, sliding the last few yards to the beach. It was a hard but not-injuring fall. The effect was like brushing her hand across a wall and inadvertently flicking a light switch.

The twinge in her belly was irrevocably sharp. She held her breath, frozen in her sprawl on the cobbles. Another, harder contraction seized and released her. Warm wetness swelled between her legs. She closed her eyes, heart and womb contracting in opposing union; endings and continuities carried on the same red tide.

She rolled onto her knees and unfastened her jeans, pulling them off, and in that momentum took off the rest of her clothes and bundled them on a rock. Sun heated the humid air. The fisted ache inside her drained into a slow stream down Trinity's thighs. She hobbled on sensitive feet over the cobbles and slick kelpy rocks, into the water, wading out until the sea lapped against knees, then waist, before standing with eyes closed, feet braced, as waves surged forward and back.

She let go of holding herself against the primordial shove and pull, giving herself to the water, floating with her face to the sky. Long, russet hair fanned out in slow, curving gestures like those of kelp fronds; blood drifted from between her legs, tendrils dispersing, pale clouds gradually borne away. She floated in the oldest of memories beyond egg and sperm. The ocean's breast rose and fell, the ebbing tide bearing Trinity away from land, beguilingly, like a thief to whom you willingly open your hands.

When she lifted her head she was far from shore. It did not alarm her—strangely, for she was cold. For some moments she treaded water, her hair sleek and sea-darkened, peering first at the shore where life stumbled and toiled among the rocks, then past the grasping arms of the bay to the open blue surge of the Minch. She gazed; a sharp breeze ruffled through time, shaping a momentary path upon the sea before waves erased it with their insistent amnesia of form. Trinity turned, swimming steadily with calculated but unfearing effort, back to land.

When she reached the black inshore rocks she hauled herself onto a shelving slab, water running from her hair and shuddering body, and pressed herself against the stone's sun-borrowed warmth. Ledges above her diverted wind, but ripples of gooseflesh swept the exposed surface of Trinity's skin as brisk air found and dried her. She closed her eyes, shivering, seeking the heated contour of being, but could not find the shape of herself against the stone. In that awkwardness she finally wept for Connell.

The sinking movement of the sun, retreating hiss of waves, calm unwondering rock, made Trinity doze, curled as though within a seashell.

She woke when there were only tide pools between her rock and the land that was ever shore. On the beach a man stood, intensely gazing at her, holding Trinity's bundle of clothes in his hands.

Trinity sat up, the water that had pooled and warmed beneath her sliding along the ribs and arm that had sided stone.

The man's regard was diffident in its curiosity but had a hungering defiance, as though he claimed territory unsettled but held sacred by some invisible race. Trinity looked back at him warily, not because of her nakedness, which did not yet seem significant in proximity to stone and wind and sea, but because he held her clothes, a half-remembered life containing clues that in their very ordinariness were beyond price.

"Old stories tell about selkies," the man called to her in a local accent, "and if a man can steal the selkie's pelt while she's in human form, she has to go with him." He looked down at the clothes in his hands and back at Trinity.

The wind stirred her hair, amplifying the stillness of her pose. The westering sunlight made her seem far away, a remoteness like the voice of surf heard in sleep.

"Old people around here say that this beach is where Duncan Ross' selkie went back to the sea. Maybe you're her?" He waited then, as though pausing for the elements to translate his request, sure as a son that it would be granted. And if not—he glanced again at the bundle in his hands, feeling precedent's righteousness.

"No," said Trinity, finding voice out of what seemed eternal silence, her mind rising to the bait of three tickling sounds: Duncan Ross' selkie. "What the sea wants is never returned."

"Then who might you be?" he asked, but Trinity would not answer until the man sighed, putting down her clothes.

He shoved his hands in his hip pockets, as he gazed regretfully at the bundle, then raised his head, squinting against the western slant of sun that framed Trinity in partisan Highland light.

"Who was the selkie?" she asked.

PART TWO

> Mi nam ròn
> Tromh'n sgàthan briste
> An dannsa shamhach
> Air thòir a bhradain….
>
> I am a selkie
> Through the broken mirror
> In silent dance
> Pursuing salmon….
>
> From *Sireadh Bradain Sicir,*
> *Seeking Wise Salmon*
> by Aonghas MacNeacail

Margaret watched her father. Duncan was seated at the cottage's table, scarred fingertips lightly resting against a cup of whisky, as if listening with his nerve endings. The peat fire smoldered and relentlessly huffed, but Margaret made no move to mend it. Murdoch was asleep on his grandparents' bed.

Duncan's bed. More than peat smoke choked Margaret, making small life's generosity to lungs and heart. Her mother dead. Margaret's breath came jagged. She quieted herself, shoulders stiff, brief rain of tears on the hard-packed dirt floor.

Duncan turned, fingers deserting the whisky cup. "Come, lass." He gathered her into his lap, though she was eleven, more mother than auntie now to three-year-old Murdoch.

David had returned from the Lowlands for his mother's funeral, full of sullen blow—even Margaret knew he lied about how he fared in Glasgow. Slum smell was unlike the weathered, fish bait-soot-byre stink of the blackhouse—a stink Margaret never thought of as poverty. David emanated sly futility, a cutthroat sneering pall that lingered in his voice, his eyes, his clothing. Her brother's movements seemed hunched and dangerous; under the weight of a corner of his mother's coffin he looked more thief than son.

Annie had concealed her illness until she collapsed and was carried to bed. She never rose again until Duncan lifted her like a bride in his arms and laid her in the coffin Jamie MacBeath had made.

Head resting on her father's shoulder, Margaret felt Duncan's sigh. She cried, her father's shirt taking up the tears, absorbing her sorrow atop the body of his own loss.

David came in, glance sliding off his father and sister, skittering over Murdoch on the box bed, rebounding to the hearth, finding sanctuary. He strode over and crouched to rearrange the peats, tilting the kettle on its soot-thickened heather rope to see what food remained. "We've a coal stove in Glasgow," he said. He scooped porridge from the kettle into a bowl and ate it standing at the hearth.

"Are you going back to the city?" his father asked.

David shoveled porridge into his mouth and shook his head. "Next month a ship's leaving Kyleakin on Skye—for Canada. Donnie MacLeod's going. I've passage fare, enough to get shot of Highland misery for good." He set his bowl aside with a clatter, obliquely observing his father. "Johanna MacLeod and me…we're marrying on Skye. The banns are posted."

Margaret stiffened, staring at her brother. "Canada? Marrying?"

Duncan had not moved, as if in stillness the shadow hand could steal no more, could no longer detect the presence of a life and what it cherished. He felt Margaret shift on his lap and restrained from tightening his clasp. "Canada has miseries, too," he said, "for those with no prospects. What do you think to do there, and with a wife?"

His son shrugged, furtive defiance that pained Duncan, relearning David's insolence, now overlaid with unlovely postures of guilt. "I'll make my way," said David. "Donnie has ideas and family there. We'll get by."

"I never knew you fancied Johanna," said Margaret, slipping from her father's lap.

David eyed the whisky jug on the table, then glanced at Margaret and half-smiled, embarrassed, truly fond of his sister, for a moment simply an awkward youth.

"I think she's bonny," Margaret offered stoutly, though she knew Johanna for an overplump, nasal girl, straight fair hair baby-fine, and blue eyes that lost color in sunlight. David had always favored bolder sorts, Margaret thought, but Johanna would make David feel clever and firm, would—for her own ease—be forgiving.

"She wants the bairn," David said, voice flat.

"Not our Murdoch! No!" Margaret blurted. "He's not hers!"

"But he is David's." Duncan's voice was soft: death's shimmering walk on the sea.

David's lips parted; he was afraid, ashamed, suddenly cognizant of his mother's absence. Knees and gut trembled; he sagged onto the long-bench.

"Rona gave him to us," Margaret raged. "You didn't want him before." Tears stormed from her.

Duncan leaned to touch her but she would not be comforted, darting to the box bed where she crawled over the coverlet, curling her bird's-wing body around Murdoch. The child never stirred, used to voices and proximity, to the protectress' breath on his cheek.

Duncan grasped the whisky cup. "Why?"

David did not look up. Already the Atlantic stretched between them. "He'll never be but motherless, fatherless

bastard here. In Canada, no one will be knowing he's not Johanna's natural son, conceived in marriage."
"For three years, you've not cared what he was. You didn't care when you begat him."
"As much gossip says he's yours as mine," David flared, instantly regretting it. Something rose from that ocean between them—burning accusation he didn't recognize as his own face, such was his terror of it. "Johanna wants him," he muttered, seeking escape. "She thinks he'll bring luck." A notion shared by many in the community: grey-eyed Murdoch a guileless mystery, smile like God's mercy. At three, already a talisman in that community of fishermen.
Duncan listened to his daughter's weeping, the conspiring fire, wind testing the thatch. He stared at his empty cup. "He's a bairn, not a bride's charm."
"He's my son."
Duncan looked up at manhood's uncertain shell. "Aye."

Trinity went to Skye. From Skye, her ancestors had departed their homeland. She needed an island, to be surrounded by sea. From the capacious hostel in the island's north she could see the wink of Gairloch's lighthouse, coded signal from her child. She didn't unpack her suitcase but felt she might never leave, held by that nightly message.
Flodigarry's crofts, below the hostel's vantage, were tucked into the green, humped land above the shore. Inland reared the Quiraing's abrupt mass—immense, gnawed cliffs and primordial landslips. She approached the heights slowly, as if knowing the futility of gaining intimacy in one lifetime—and the necessity of trying. Daily she broached this elemental fortress, heedless of harsh weather and moods that would rather pace unexposed behind locked doors. Trinity—successful American author—had not written a word of prose since arriving in Scotland. After three weeks of walking the Quiraing she began the story of Duncan Ross' selkie.

When pen touched paper Trinity's mind found channel, like the musician lifting hands to the keyboard, the actress when the cameras begin to roll. Time broadened. The story eddied into sensuality's articulation.

She worked at a dining room table by a window where she could glance out at cloud-harried light over sea and headlands, tides withdrawing to expose seal-like boulders, water again covering the rocks as waves drove in, assailing the cliffs. Seabirds dove, white plumes of spray flaring from the surface; above the hills kestrels hovered—pennants in the wind. Flodigarry Island, moored offshore, floated in treeless patience.

One morning Trinity rode the bus to the southern end of Skye, along narrow, syncopated roads. Arriving at the Gaelic college in Sleat, she asked the Welsh poet in residence, "What about selkies?"

He shrugged; loaned her books of folk tales. In the island's libraries she scanned hushed parish records and unruly clan histories. The only trace of Duncan Ross' family was on a passenger list for the Marian's 1860 voyage to Nova Scotia; on it were the names of David and Johanna Ross and their child, Murdoch. She found mention of Duncan Ross in reports of the Greenyards' battle; she wrote to her father, asking if he'd ever heard of a mystery regarding Duncan's tenure in Gairloch.

Her father's reply, typically dry: I inherited Duncan's fiddle but no mystery other than why the stubborn fool didn't emigrate. Are you re-creating his folly with your current duration on the auld sod?

At fifteen Margaret was as tall as she would get. Bonny wee girl, Duncan thought, watching her remove shoes and stockings at the Sunday Stone, stopping place between cottage and kirk where women donned or doffed their precious footwear. Margaret had her father's dark-haired good looks, if not his reassuring size. She was quick, disconcerting, fearless. Duncan sometimes shivered, seeing her as fairy-like.

"Why the bright smiles for Calum Ban's cousin from Skye?" Duncan asked, mildly for a father.

Margaret hopped down from the stone. They resumed walking. "Angus MacKinnon tells merry stories. Why should I not smile?"

"Flirting, he is, and you far too young for such attentions from a grown man." Duncan paced along slowly, his stride appreciating the luxury of solid ground.

"Ach, Da, shall we not invite him to tea, then?"

"We shall not," affirmed Duncan.

They walked in silence a ways.

"It's been a lonely house with your mother and brother and the bairn gone." He looked down at his daughter. "You're my merry story."

Trinity dreamed kelpie dreams—shorelines and wind, receding figures, headlands named for drowned fishermen, empty blackhouses and crowded ships. Sheep. She stared out the bus window as she rode the twenty miles into Portree for shopping, tangled in those dreams, testing one plot thread after another, knots obsessively created and unraveled, the landscape a parallel universe. At the hostel the staff grew used to seeing Trinity at the window table, her oblivion oracular in its attention to invisible realms. The staff, Colin from Birmingham, Morag who did the cleaning, treated her with indulgence, as though she had a salutary illness. They stopped asking how long she would be staying.

Tourist season unfolded in the Isles: rental cars crunched over the gravel car park, feet thudded on stairs, cameras greedily consumed sunrises over Staffin Bay. The kitchen emptied and filled with meal tides—richly choking smells of frying fish and bacon, the restaurant odor of ubiquitous Italian fast food. Travel brochures were strewn like abandoned poker hands amid biscuit crumbs, chocolate wrappers, and half-empty mugs of cold coffee.

Trinity, indefensibly territorial, resented the influx. She took her notebooks into the Quiraing and wrote in shielings where sheep and buzzards tended to the business of survival, ignoring her.

It was a chill, wet summer, but tourists didn't come to Scotland to sunbathe. The island's small capitol town of Portree swelled with visitors—queues at the bakery, the bank, the Co-op; Somerled Square littered with rucksacked pedestrians consulting bus timetables, eager, anxious, glazed. Avoiding crowds, Trinity gravitated to the north end's extremities, where she pondered the sea between Skye and the Western Isles.

"Looking for Blue Men?" a voice—Scottish, at least—punctured her reverie one afternoon.

Trinity looked up, recognizing the busking piper taking a break from offering tunes for visitors. He managed to appear comfortable in formal piping regalia. "Blue Men?"

"Wicked riddlers—aquatic," he said, gesturing at the blue expanse before them. "Said to frequent the Minch."

"Do pipe tunes appeal to them?"

He smiled slightly. "Tourist coins are all I'm after." His gaze was tolerant. "I've seen you around. A long holiday?"

"Something of the sort."

"I'm Alie MacLeod." He leaned to offer his hand.

She briefly clasped it. "Trinity Ross."

He inspected her, blue eyes interested, his midthirties, bony Celtic face elongated by an impressive rectangular brush of beard, like a harrier's tail.

"Named after a mountain range," Trinity added, used to the necessity.

"And here I am merely called for all the first sons before me," Alie said with insincere envy.

"Pipers as well?"

"Some of them."

"From around here?"

He raised his brows at her persistence, not seeing it was her defense. "Some of them, though I grew up near Kinlochewe, then the Black Isle, before moving here. My father is from Skye, but my mother's people are from Wester Ross—MacKenzies from over by Loch Maree."

Trinity contracted around the place names. "Do you like Skye?" she asked, making space.

"Oh, aye. I live over that hill there." He gestured behind. "Kilmuir. Plenty here to inspire, if the drink doesn't get me. Some pipers manage both—music and drink—but not me. I lost out to the whisky for ten years, but now I'm getting the music back." He gazed down at her, unembarrassed.

"Are there selkies in the Minch along with Blue Men?"

Alie studied her. "Who knows? I've never seen one, just seals." He looked over his shoulder toward the road. "Another coach. See you sometime?"

"No doubt."

Trinity passed the piper later as she skirted the ruins of Duntulm Castle. He stood beside the cairn with its Gaelic-English inscriptions honoring MacArthur pipers: *The world will end, but music and love endureth.* Trinity dropped a pound coin into the instrument case at Alie's feet. The piper winked, no break in the pibroch.

The sea surged, coldly seductive, green under grey clouds and grey-toothed wind. Margaret came down from the shielings, shawl tightly wrapped against the blow, and firmly shut the cottage door behind her. She stood a moment in the gloom, listening to the muffled roar of wind and sea, then began sweeping and redding-up the cottage, affirming habitation. She awoke the fire, adding peats, and heated water to boil potatoes, preparing for her father's return.

It was July, but raw, and in July, cold was an injustice. Margaret, doing an adult's work, usually dreamed a girl's dreams while she labored, but not this day. Chill locked her into severe moment, congealing at the knock on the blackhouse door.

Behind her uncle stood five of Watson's six-man crew. Margaret had no ear for their words, hearing only the silence of the man they carried, and the water running from him onto the hard ground.

Kinlochewe was a long walk from North Erradale. Margaret found the bard's cottage at last, her inquiries sounding thin but loud after a speechless day. There had been days of little speech, many tears, as though grief would drown her. It had taken more than grief to drown her father; she held to this as she walked, bearing her few clothes, her father's fiddle, her mother's hairbrush, in a bundle on her back. A food packet half-filled the pail she shifted from hand-to-hand as the miles passed.

Three locks of hair were entwined in a seashell in her pocket: the rich, dark hair of her father's, the modest brown of her mother's, and Murdoch's fine auburn curl, all wound round with one tantalizing strand of Rona's, gleaned years before from the sea-woman's comb. Margaret had nothing of David but the Nova Scotia address taken from his last letter—his only letter in four years of absence. *We are well*, he had written. *Johanna is pregnant. I expect to have work soon.* Hardly a mention of Murdoch.

The bard was home. He opened the door at Margaret's knock and beckoned her in, taking pipe from mouth and gesturing with it to the cottage's only chair, greeting her courteously despite the late hour and the impropriety of her arrival. He gave her tea like an honored guest, and waited for her to speak, an uncommonly forbearing man.

"I am Margaret Ross of North Erradale," she said, holding the teacup in both hands. "I remember how you came to see our Rona when I was a young girl."

"Aye," he said, his gaze sharpening, "I do recall that." His full beard against his chest reminded Margaret of heath on the moor, quivering at the wind's news. For a moment she held the memory of scurrying sheep and mild-eyed cattle, but her mind flinched from the image of her father kneeling, gently parting the heather to reveal the secret world of orchid and bird's egg.

"Margaret Ross," the bard said, "what has befallen? You've come far, and by your luggage look to be going farther yet."

"Not so far as the others, our Rona, Mum and Da, David with our Murdoch." Her hands trembled; her tea gave a worried shiver. "Have you heard aught of Rona?" she asked, spilling her purpose. "Have you heard where she might be?"

MacKenzie set his pipe on the bench and ran both hands once up and down his face as though to erase the desperate sadness of her question. "No, lass. I've not heard."

County Mayo was a poor place. Fin O'Sullivan was suited to it: born there, raised there, destitute as only an Irish Catholic those days could be, likewise as astute. He had watched his older brother die, his mother die; had found his father dead on the roadside. He never knew what became of the rest of the family—three sisters, another brother: everyone evicted. A haze surrounded it. Orphaned in the winter of 1853, at age seven, Fin remained in that dark haze until emerging from poorhouse and fosterage at age sixteen into acute independence. He had survived where most did not; instead of abject, Fin burned.

Trinity wanted an origin for Duncan's selkie. In her story, she called the sea-woman Fiona, but where could she have come from? Born on some seal-populous reef? Conjured from saline magic? Merely a dream, a fantasy, a bard's tale? Or a deluded woman wandering into the sea? Trinity couldn't shake the feeling that whatever she decided would shortchange truth and fail to honor ancestral verity.

Her story faltered, turned in on itself like the cool, pale curve of a conch shell, its interior hidden, sea-filled.

She set notebooks aside, the balk temporary. She was, in this, professional: opening would occur once she stopped hounding the muse. Birmingham Colin, the hostel warden, invited her on a foray to Storr Lochs, where he regularly tried his luck with a fly rod despite want of the requisite fishing permit. Trinity startled him by accepting. "I'll wander while you tempt fate," she said.

The lochs reclined along the single-track road halfway between Portree and Flodigarry. Inland from the lochs towered the buttress of Storr Mountain with its famed upthrust of crumbly basalt, euphemized in English as The Old Man of Storr; in Gaelic, forthrightly named Storr's Penis. A fine rain was falling when they parked the hostel van and climbed out, Colin equipping himself with rod and pork pie; Trinity tightening her rain hood and slipping an apple into her pocket.

"Hour and a half?" Colin suggested."

Trinity nodded. "Good luck." She struck off seaward, away from the intimidating loom of the mountain, along the single-track road. Crossing the bridge over the dam, she left the lochs behind, then halted, seeing Rona's baffling profile stretched along the grey blur where sky met sea. No one there but the military, Colin had told her, a submarine station. The island looked both mysterious and violated; no trees, only rounded rock like a disjointed series of vertebrae, silent, exposed, but enigmatic. It had once been populated.

"That's where my Fiona came from," Trinity murmured. She stared at the isle until immobility chilled her, then turned and walked back toward the van, gnawing the apple.

Margaret paced the pier at Portree, as though the thousands of steps bringing her to Skye had been insufficient for decision. Had it been a matter solved by rational exercise, she would've stayed at Gairloch to begin with, absorbed into a MacBeath household, marrying or not when the time came. Duncan's boat was hers, his nets and gear, his five cows, ten sheep, and two white ponies.

Rona's silence, though total, had never lacked presence. Margaret's compulsion to seek the sea-woman perhaps was hope that in that presence other silences would cease their deathly emptiness: the fiddle would sing; she would hear the soft rasp of the brush as it stroked her mother's hair. Duncan had brushed his wife's hair every night Margaret could remember: it was her measure of how best a man loves. Sleep no longer easily approached without that hushing rhythm to invite it. Silence was a desertion of touchstones.

She instinctively knew there was no touchstone in David. He had lost his Gaelic recognition of those features of personal landscape identifying wholeness: features lying submerged in him like a drowned island. Murdoch could swim but Margaret could not. She paced the pier as if bracing for a suicidal leap into the tide.

"I declare—Margaret Ross! And looking so desperate! Where's your da?"

Margaret spun. It was Angus MacKinnon of the merry tales, a sack over one shoulder, bunnet tipped back, hand on his hip. Decision's net had drawn him, Margaret was certain. "My father is drowned. I'm making my own way now."

"Ach, no. Sorry for such poor news," Angus said, eyeing her bundle and pail. "I would've thought he'd of left you a bit more...."

"Plenty he left me," she flared, temper and grief. "Croft and boat, sheep and kye, plenty and fair. I came away, is all. I came away."

Angus shook his head. "'Tis daft, girl. Were you minded to go over the waves?"

"I may."

He grinned. Her tone so confident, standing in her rough brown clothes and waif's bundle. Pert, she was. "No ships sailing this week, young miss. Why not stop with my sister

Catriona a while, sort things out before jumping ahead. She could use a hand with the bairns."

When he was seventeen Fin joined the Irish Republican Brotherhood. His family thereafter bided easier in the Afterworld—this Fin knew. And O'Sullivans to come straightened resolute if ethereal shoulders in manifestation's anteroom. The IRB quickened Fin's talents for survival, conceived in the poorhouse's bitter womb. His ferocity smoldered, but self-control made Fin a cold lover and opaque, if loyal, friend. He saw himself as a weapon belonging to the IRB and honed his functionality accordingly.

Fin's body was marked by malnutrition's thefts and the poorhouse's punishments. He was smaller than he might have been; his bones were weak, his teeth deplorable, his chest pinched. But his face was that of an archangel, incorruptible; and his hands moved with surpassing intelligence. If humor brushed him bitterly and foolishness not at all, there was an unexpected sensitivity in Fin's touch that bordered on cherishing. But any arena where the best of him could've found expression was voided in 1869. Fin was caught gunrunning, charged with treason-felony, and sentenced to fifteen years' hard labor.

Another Mayo man, Michael Davitt, born the same year as Finn, his family evicted from their Straid hovel when Michael was four, was imprisoned on a like charge in 1871. The Davitt family had moved to Lancashire after eviction. Michael lost his right arm laboring in a Haslingden cotton mill when he was twelve. Never a husky boy—tall but close-knit, quietly intense—Michael early learned a man's fortitude; he'd begun the mill job at age nine.

Second oldest of the Davitt's five children, Michael received the benefits of a Wesleyan education due to the recommendation of an idealistic parish priest who believe in religious harmony. Study of Irish history irresistibly led to fenianism. The Irish Republican Brotherhood had formed in 1858 to overthrow Britain's oppressive authority; Davitt joined in 1865 when he was nineteen. For two years he combined newspaper work with fenian activities. Unlike Fin, however, Davitt's military participation in the IRB was limited to an attempt to seize arms stored in Chester Castle. In 1868 Davitt resigned from Cockcrofts' newspaper and became the IRB's organizing secretary in England and Scotland, a position inevitably involving him in arms smuggling to Ireland. He was arrested in Paddington Station in London, accused of trafficking guns in barrels of apples, convicted of treason-felony, and imprisoned in England. Conditions were grim. For a one-armed man, the assignment of stone breaking and crushing meat bones for manure was sadistic. Fin fared little better in his Irish prison. Both men were released in 1877 following an amnesty campaign, but it would be another two years before they met.

Margaret studied the slope of Ben Lee, the now-private graze that had been used in common since clanship days. Margaret was a newcomer to Braes, the hill country eight miles south of Portree, but her husband's people had long tenure there. The year of her marriage, 1865, was also the year Lord MacDonald's factor made Ben Lee's slopes the leased property of a single sheep farmer.

Braes crofters were dismayed. Angus, bringing the news home to Margaret, shrugged in his careless way and said, "I'll sign on a Lewis boat, or a Wick one for that matter. There's never been luck raising beasts and only bad luck raising crops. I'll fare better on the water where luck has room to find a canny man."

Angus was nearly thirty, Margaret a mere sixteen; nonetheless, Margaret was the more mature. Merriment came easily to Angus, and sudden temper as well. He was shortsighted and stormy, mercurial and maddening. Despite a well-shaped body that adapted without strain to the moment's demands, he seemed perpetually on the brink of catastrophe.

Margaret gave him pause. She was sprite-sized but purposeful—a swallow in flight. Her father's fiddle remained silent; she brushed her own hair; but Angus wooed her with droll tales, disarming touch, odd evocative gifts brought from sea and moor; and with his refusal to kowtow to the lairds.

The potato crop had failed in 1864, as had the winter fishing in herring and ling: rough weather, a lean year, proprietors having to advance seed and meal to distressed crofters. Typhus swept the townships, though Skye was largely spared the TB plague of the mainland. There was a dearth of social music on Skye as well. No ceilidhs. Only psalms sung line by line after the kirk precenter. Margaret hungered for the flirt of a country tune, for the head-back swirl of a quickstep reel. Loss of family and loss of music merged in her mind, a silence Angus' irreverent stories did not dispel.

After their first year of marriage, Angus was often away. In spring he jigged for herring during the brief west coast season. In July he migrated to the North Sea, crewing aboard the huge fleet of herring boats out of Caithness. Autumn found him on the great inland hunting estates, where he worked as a deerstalker or fishing ghillie, rarely lasting more than one season on any estate; though skillful, Angus lacked deference. In winter he pursued whitefish with Western Islanders in the Minch. Many Skyemen went south for seasonal jobs, working the harvests of Lowland farms or road building; women also migrated, laboring at fish curing stations or as servants or farm workers. West coast Highlanders and Islanders, by necessity, had become a mobile population.

But Margaret bided in Braes, tending to their six sheep, one pony, two stirks, all bought from the sale of Duncan's stock in Gairloch. Angus plowed, but it was Margaret who planted, cultivated, and harvested potatoes, oats, turnips, and a bit of barley their one arable acre accommodated. There was not enough land for crop rotation. Selling stirks each year paid the rent—they couldn't grow enough fodder to overwinter cattle. And every year, Margaret sold two or three wedders. There was always debt, never security. If they planted too early in a wet, cold year, crops were lost; if they waited too cautiously, crops did not ripen. Fishing could fail, blight could strike; they lived beneath disaster's shadow.

But Margaret bided, still dreaming, though as year chased year the dreams weathered in thin Braes soil.

She wrote to David, telling him of her marriage, her life on Skye. He never answered. She tried to imagine Murdoch eight years old, thirteen, sixteen. Year chased year, and Margaret remained childless. Perhaps Angus was not home enough; perhaps barrenness was a maternal legacy or a loss at one with Murdoch's absence and Margaret's severance from kin. She bided, busy and lonely, and never word of Rona.

In the autumn of 1874, when Margaret turned twenty-five, Angus brought home from Inverness a copy of *The Highlander*, tossing the newspaper on the table and shrugging out of his coat. "Something to occupy your evenings when I'm away again. I've brought jam and tea for you as well. Have you a kiss for me, Maggie lass?"

Trinity paid her hostel bill week by week. The last Saturday in July she stopped at the reception window after breakfast, seeing it open, Colin perusing the booking diary on the counter.

"You should about own that room by now," Colin said, as she plunked her money on top of the diary.

"That's an idea."

"Take it up with Archie," Colin sidestepped, referring to the hostel owner.

"Will crowds get worse in August?"

Colin nodded, looking pleased. "Our busiest month. That twin room you're keeping to yourself is worth gold—don't be surprised if Archie bumps up the price."

"Thanks for the warning." She surveyed the booking diary upside down, scanning the column listing the guests' countries of origin, arrested by a telltale NI. "Who's in twelve?" she asked.

"Twelve? Bloke from Belfast on the crew redoing the island's electrical lines. His name's Chris. Why?"

Trinity had no reasonable answer. "Just wondered," she said.

Colin looked dubious—idle questions weren't her style. Trinity backed away, bumped into a Frenchwoman, apologized, retreating upstairs. She wasn't ready for a Belfast accent in the kitchen.

Morag, hoovering Trinity's room, switched off the machine when she saw Trinity, saying, "Thought you'd be longer downstairs. I'm about finished here."

Trinity sat on the bed, looking blankly at Morag, trying to marshal a congenial response.

"You all right?" Morag rarely engaged guests, but Trinity was practically a resident, and tidy. "You look turned on end."

"Nothing, really." She watched the older woman neatly coil the electrical cord. "Wrestling with myself."

Morag shook her head. "The hardest fights, those. But you're clever—all that book writing. You'll figure it out."

"Clever." She grimaced. "What I need is common sense—practicality."

"What color would life be then?" Morag whipped her dust cloth over the windowsill and trundled the vacuum cleaner into the hall.

Trinity holed up in her room. Instead of using the kitchen she bought snack food from Colin, which amused him, or went hungry, which irritated her. At midday on

Monday, assuming the Irishman well away at work, she ventured into the kitchen to cook a decent meal.

The dining room was nearly deserted, hostel guests off hiking, castle touring, shopping. Two Kiwis leaned over cups of tea, decoding the Tarbert ferry schedule. A Dutch youth coddled a hangover on the sofa. Trinity busied herself with pots and pans, assembling something substantial if not memorable. A voice at her back stiffened her.

"Sorry. Could I have that tin opener when you're done?" asked a masculine voice—Midlands.

Trinity turned, passing the requested implement, pulse still jumping.

Crazy, she reprimanded herself, sitting down with her food, doggedly relaxing.

Afterward she washed, dried, and put away her dishes, moving mechanically. There was an unreasonable ache in her womb. She went upstairs and zipped on her windbreaker, then left the hostel.

Walking was an addiction, exertion compelling deeper breath, wider view. Reminder of a living world: weather, season, stone underfoot, prevailing wind, tireless sea. Walking sorted if not healed her. It made her body lean instead of slender, her smallness covert, features weather-honed and watchful—no longer American hothouse naked.

She veered too late at the sight of the Hydro van parked on the roadside half a mile south of the hostel. One of the linemen leaned on the door, talking to the men inside. He turned his head at Trinity's approach, then straightened, pushing back from the door with a laborer's economy of effort. He was not tall, instead had a condensed strength. Unremarkably blond short hair suited the tight build and intense impersonal voice with its Belfast signature.

"Hello," he said, eyeing her. "I've seen you in the hostel at night in the corridors. A ghost. Glad the light of day hasn't driven you to your coffin."

Trinity tarried, hands fisted in her pockets. "Don't be too sure that's not where I'm headed. Might be best to wear a lump of garlic around your neck just in case."

Laughter from inside the van. Trinity resumed walking, hearing a fragment of joke about garlic and sex appeal, missing the Irishman's retort. *No big deal*, she told the flush over her body, the tension in her gut and shoulders.

She cut away from the road, crossing boggy grazeland to reach the shore, walking until the surf erased chagrin.

Alie MacLeod overtook her on the path leading past the pub on her way home. "Buy you a drink?" the piper offered. "The pub is quiet this time of day. I've noticed you're not one for crowds."

"Thought you were off drink."

Alie smiled. "I go there for the *craic* and to meet women, not for the whisky." The craic: socializing.

Trinity glanced at the man striding beside her, his everyday humor and courage. "All right. Thanks."

The pub was as promised, the bartender reading a newspaper, intermittently taking in the football match on television. It looked to be the same match glimpsed on any screen at any time in Europe. Alie carried their soft drinks to a corner table, where an unrushed assessment continued.

"You're a writer?"

Trinity nodded, sipping her ginger beer.

"Published?"

She nodded again.

"Obviously not an investigative journalist."

She smiled, setting down her glass. "Sorry. Rusty social skills."

He studied her, then began talking about an estate in Duirnish, in northwest Skye; old MacLeod clan land presently owned by a German pop star, now up for sale. "Seventy-two hundred acres. A group of us, crofters on the estate and others with family ties to that land, are talking about buying out the estate owner, buying the whole thing as a community."

"Where would you get the money?" Trinity asked. "Busking can't be all that lucrative."

"That's the rub," the piper admitted. "We're drawing up a funding proposal—approaching LEC, Highland Council, a few other government agencies. We need five to eight hundred thousand quid, though even if we gather the money there's always the chance some rich bastard will outbid us."

"Your father's people used to live there?"

"Driven off it in the 1800s. Clearances. My father's from Glendale."

Trinity nodded. Same old story, but with a possible new ending—reclamation. "What will the community do with the estate if they get it? More crofts?"

"Partly," Alie said, pleased at her interest. He leaned back in the chair, a lanky man beginning to thicken at the center, unpretentious, with a musician's confident hands, a piper's good-natured dignity. "There's not much of a living to be made in crofting—when it comes to livestock, anyway. We're thinking of diverse use but in keeping with traditional values—and environmentalism."

"Are you the grant writer?"

Alie grinned. "You like my phraseology? No, I'm not the writer. We've been consulting Michael Lovat, a solicitor who helped with a couple other community buy-outs. He's giving us general advice but doesn't have time to do the grants and proposals." He leaned forward. "How about you, though? You're a writer."

Trinity blinked and stammered, displaying little of the articulate brilliance the piper was courting. "Geez, Alie.... I'm not even a resident. I don't know the convolutions of agency politics, how stuff operates here...."

"We'll coach you. Don't you realize the history being made? The defeat of the toff's tyranny?" He smiled, trying to spark her. "Don't you want to be more than a tourist? Didn't you once have family here?"

Her floundering reply was snuffed by the entrance of the line crew, local men except for the Irishman. Two remained at the bar after ordering; Chris and the fourth man took their Guinnesses nearer the television, nodding as they passed the corner table.

"Stays at the hostel, doesn't he?" Alie asked, noting her discomfort at seeing Chris.

She nodded.

"Had a bad encounter with him?"

She shook her head, finding her voice. "No, no. It's nothing personal."

Alie raised his brows. "You dislike the Irish? Come now. I thought Americans these days loved the Irish."

"No, not that either! It has nothing to do with liking or disliking. It's just...something I don't want to talk about, OK?"

"Of course. Can I get you a refill?"

Trinity felt like a fool. "Thanks, no. I should be going." She reached for her jacket. "Listen, I'll think about the grant writing."

Alie stood, helping her arm find its sleeve, a gallant man. "Ceilidh on Friday at Kilmuir. Might you come?"

"Doubtful."

He sighed. "We're having a meeting about the Ferinurchar estate on Wednesday night. Might you at least come to that? I'll give you a ride, no strings attached."

Trinity zipped her jacket, attention straying to the Irishman. "All right. Sure. Wednesday? What time?"

"I'll pick you up at about seven." He smiled benignly. "Bring a notebook."

Reading John Murdoch's editorials in *The Highlander*, Margaret felt Duncan at her shoulder, and Annie, too, as she had been at Greenyards. Murdoch wrote of the need to abolish landlordism itself, not just its abuses. He held that land was not a commodity to serve greed. Murdoch voiced truths long silenced, ignored, banished, confounded. Gaels had been unprepared to defend their way of life, unprepared for betrayal from their own chiefs. Never had they known how to explain themselves to outsiders. The Gaels had no manifesto.

John Murdoch had seasoned himself in Irish nationalist politics and agrarian reform. Moving from Ireland's hotbed to the smolder of the Highlands, Murdoch offered an alternative to *The Daily Liar* and its pro-landlord platitudes. In Braes the crofters, now including families cleared from Sqoirebreac, Torra-micheig, and even Kilmuir and Staffin, eyed the broad slopes of Ben Lee and the congested townships below and collectively muttered.

Denied work at the sporting estates, Angus resigned himself to an autumn of smearing. One man could smear up to twenty sheep a day. The stink of the butter, tar, and grease concoction the smearers rubbed into the fleeces to protect sheep from vermin lingered on Angus' hands for months. The rancidity mingled with the blackhouse's reek of peat smoke, sour milk, and chicken dung.

"It doesn't matter," said Margaret, but it drove Angus back to the boats and the restless, clean sea wind.

"When will you be home?" Margaret asked, watching him pack his necessities.

"When will you be giving us a bairn?" Angus countered. "You'd miss me less with young ones afoot."

"Catriona's bairns are underfoot as often as not, though I suppose they've grown too big to fit under a foot like mine." In truth, the youngest was twelve. Seemed but a day since she'd had them on knee and under arm, as well as underfoot.

"I'm nearing forty," Angus reminded her. "It needs be soon or never for making me a father."

"I've heard...." Margaret stopped. No point.

"You've heard what?"

"Nothing. A Portree woman with a son the image of you. Gossip." She turned away, knowing his ways. There was no joy in watching a man lie.

Angus slapped shut his carryall. "Only fools listen to other folks claik." He ran his fingers through spiky hair, one of the few men Margaret knew who, like Duncan, went beardless. "Are you making complaint of me, Maggie?"

She shook her head. "Would you bring another of John Murdoch's newspapers when you come back next?"

He shrugged, amused. "Wouldnae rather a hair ribbon?"

Margaret thought of her mother crumpled in her own blood at Greenyards, of Duncan manacled to a cart. "No. Murdoch's paper."

1879 and 1880 were years of downpour and meager harvest in Ireland—years of near famine. County Mayo was a land of misery. In April of '79, the rent-racked tenants on the Bourke estate near Irishtown were informed of impending eviction—eleven more families to swell the tide of homelessness.

On April 20, Fin O'Sullivan joined seven thousand of his hedge-schooled countrymen attending a public meeting called by Michael Davitt in Irishtown. "You organize the audience, and I'll organize the speakers," Davitt told Fin's Mayo delegation.

Thomas Daly and Pat Ruane addressed an audience that overflowed the field outside Irishtown. John Ferguson from Glasgow also spoke, as did Thomas Brennan of Dublin, MP O'Connor Power, and others. The theme was the land for the people.

Directly following this demonstration of resolve, the Bourke eviction notices were withdrawn and rents reduced by twenty-five percent. "The tenant farmers have a right to assert themselves as men," the estate owner belatedly concluded.

In June, another meeting was organized, this time in Mayo's Westport, and with this, Davitt persuaded Charles Stuart Parnell to throw his political weight into the agrarian reform movement. Parnell feared secret societies; identifying himself with agrarian agitation was risky. Before 1879, Irish politicians had never organized support in parish branches because of the danger that leaders would be held responsible for capricious branch actions. But once committed, Parnell was outspoken.

At the Westport meeting, standing on a manmade mound in the rain, he declared, "A fair rent is a rent the tenant can pay according to the times. You must show them that you intend to hold a firm grip on your homesteads and lands."

Meetings proliferated. The Mayo Land League was birthed by Davitt in August at the James Dalys Hotel in Castlebar. It stood two months on its own before absorbed into the National Land League, inaugurated in Dublin with Parnell as president, Davitt its secretary. The massed strength of passive resistance had begun.

Fin, his fenian credentials suiting him to the task at hand, quickly made himself useful to Davitt. The two Mayo men had much in common, and an affinity despite Fin's harboring a violence not found in Davitt. Years later Davitt would comment, "When one finds oneself in prison at age twenty-four, bereft of everything that endears us to life, and surrounded by every condition of existence that could excite and keep alive passion and resentment, it is a hard and unequal struggle to conquer the spirit of hate and revenge." Davitt had conquered hate: Fin was fueled by it, but the two understood each other.

Understood—and quarreled often: Davitt was unhappy with the fenians' lack of tolerance; Fin uncompromising, if devious. The fenians were defunct as a military threat, their dreams smashed, but they continued to meet secretly in the hills. In 1880 Davitt was expelled from the Supreme Council of the IRB for involving fenian forces in Parnell's parliamentary campaign.

But Fin stayed in both the IRB and the Land League. Davitt's vision offered a concrete path—something besides waiting and clandestine military drills. Half of Mayo's population had been lost to famine and eviction: Fin needed action.

Davitt believed in constitutional means. He saw landlordism as the linchpin in a system that had become an embarrassment to Britain; the English no longer needed landlords for control of Ireland. Catholic emancipation had voided the landlords' political clout—though the landlords still controlled 122,000 acres of Ireland, mainly in Leinster, Kerry, and Limerick. "The key to national freedom is the land question," Davitt repeatedly asserted.

At six-feet tall, Davitt towered over Fin. In spite of his missing arm, Davitt was strong and vigorous. His swarthy complexion and deep-set dark eyes, emphatic features, and high forehead topped by thin dark hair, made him a striking figure. Fin, pale skin like a prison memory, clean shaven in contrast to Davitt's beard, small, cold-eyed, with a black tangle of curls females of all ages compulsively touched, was not a man you would set political store by, but one you knew would give every drop of his Irish blood for your right to self-determination.

1880 brought a fourth year of dismal harvests. Famine's agony stalked; wholesale evictions threatened in Connacht and Munster. South Connemara, in County Galway, was divided by Cuan an Fhir Mhoir into a plethora of creek-bordered islands, a treeless desolate land, and, on the first of January, 1880, was even less cheerful a place than usual. A tenant's son in Carraroe, in the heart of Connemara's hinterland, had married without his landlord's permission, and the rent on his family holdings was promptly raised five pounds as a penalty.

Another tenant was fined ten pounds when his two sons took brides and were given an outhouse in which to live. One of the final straws was the case of Andrew Conneely and his brother. Andrew had his rent doubled. His brother, on an adjacent holding, had lagged on his rent after an especially punishing year. Andrew was informed that if he didn't pay both his own inflated rent and his brother's arrears, evictions would ensue.

Rain had flattened the pitiful crops. Returns from barley, oats, and wheat were negligible. Worst of all, the potatoes failed. The rent-racking atop this ignited Connemara's revolt, and on the first day of the new year Fin traversed the Connemara creeks to see how the tenants were faring.

Outside Carraroe he found roads vandalized and barricades raised. The women were in an uproar, their men watching. Fin snaked to the front of the crowd gathering around a process-server who was approaching the house of a Mrs. Maickle. As Fin watched, the process-server was set upon by women and children obstructing access to the Maickle dwelling. Fin saw the officer go down, and his papers shredded.

Policemen bulled through toward the house. Fin vaulted the barricade and ran forward as Mrs. Maickle herself dashed out bearing a large burning turf, with which she attacked the District Police Inspector. The inspector shouted, bayonets snapped into place, and the police charged. Fin barged into the melee, women screaming around him, children shrieking at the sudden cut of steel, blood streaming down famine-whipped bodies.

At this, the men were goaded. One man, impaled in the onrush, collapsed at Fin's back with a wild cry. His fall jolted Fin forward into a reddened blade. Fin knew a searing moment of eye contact with fear, then it was pain, blinding, more irrevocable than love.

Trinity jerked awake from a smothering dream. She heard drunk Aussie voices in the hall. She groaned, not knowing why she stayed on at the hostel, in Scotland, in space not her own. What claim did it have, this restless, stubborn inertia?

She sat up. A door slammed, muffled laughter. She picked up her clock to peer at the glowing digitals: 1:23 AM. Trinity sighed, swung her legs out of bed and stood, groping for her sweat pants and pulling them on. She had slept in T-shirt and socks. The Aussies had left the bathroom light on. Trinity squinted in the brightness as she went to pee, then squinted at herself in the mirror over the sink, unimpressed. Nonetheless, she went downstairs into the kitchen, thinking a cup of yogurt might smooth her mood. She was no longer sleepy; maybe she'd write.

The dining room was occupied: an American girl strummed the hostel guitar, her companion boozily crooning a John Denver song, his German accent incongruous. At the window table, Chris sat with a cup of tea and the sports section of *The Scotsman*.

"It's the ghost," he said when she walked past with her yogurt. "Have a chair." He pushed out the one opposite him with his foot, effectively impeding passage. "Just the kind of food I'd expect a ghost to eat," he continued, inspecting the yogurt while she seated herself, "cold, white, and slithery. My name's Chris Docherty, by the way."

Trinity began eating, briefly wishing she'd brushed her hair before coming down, then lapsing into her prevailing social indifference. Chris didn't seem to mind one-sided conversation. He didn't ask the usual hosteler's questions: Where are you from? Where have you been? Where are you going next? How long have you been here? He talked about how he best liked curry prepared, how Calum had behaved at the pub that night, how Alison had reacted, and how he missed fishing in the calming river by his father's house in Donegal.

"Donegal?" asked Trinity. "I was told you're from Belfast; your accent sounds Belfast."

"Ah, she speaks. A ghost with a voice. You hear Belfast because that's where I've lived with me mum since I was six. And how would you be knowing so provincial a thing as a Belfast accent?" He studied her keenly, as if finally uncovering an explanation for his idle but unerring interest in her.

She forced herself to placidly finish her yogurt. "Knew a man from Belfast."

"Which part?"

"West." She gently set the spoon in the bowl as if demonstrating how the Irishman should treat her fragile psyche. "Sevastopol Street is what he mentioned. His people were from Mayo." That much Connell had told her when he asked her to come to Ireland. "He's dead now."

"I live on Falk Road, same district. Like to tell me this man's name?"

"Connell," she said, tasting the sound like long-denied whisky on an alcoholic's tongue. "Connell O'Sullivan."

Chris stared unwaveringly at her. "O'Sullivan's not dead," he said finally. "Not the Connell O'Sullivan I know, anyway. 'Twas Rory Keenan died. Connell survived, though not by much. He's in Long Kesh now. It was reported amiss at first—don't you read the papers?"

Trinity sat motionless, like a cartoon character when hit with a hammer, in the frozen moment before disintegration into a thousand shards. Chris did not apologize for the shock, neither did he savor it; he simply watched her, stillness the only appropriate participation. The singing in the other corner of the room went on, punctuated by laughter.

Trinity stood. "Thanks," she said.

Fin dreamed of famine, evil fiery dreams coming from the gut. He dreamed in a fever of pain and woke to the feel of Mary Ronayhe's patient, bony hands changing his bandage. "What day is it?" he croaked, not liking vulnerable unconsciousness; not liking how awake felt, either, but preferring it, knowing he was alive.

"'Tis Monday in Carraroe and Monday where you're from as well, I expect," the weary woman told him, finishing with the bandage and offering him water.

Two days lost. "What happened? Were many hurt?"

"Many for certain, and most of them female. A bit laggard, our men, but now there's all of two thousand of them roused and gathered, and more in reserve. They'll cut the bridges if the bastards try serving more papers. Nearly two hundred fifty police here now, and it's a hungry time they're having."

"No one's taking their money?"

Mrs. Ronayhe shook her head. She almost smiled.

Margaret woke alone. Not how she'd imagined married life would be—no man, no bairns. She lacked her brother's capacity for self-pity, but sometimes saw herself from a distance. Not as others saw her, not in discernment of personality—bright feather amid the grey—but as a life moving like a cat's-paw wind over the sea. Taking a path as fleeting and insubstantial as it was singular and contiguous with all else.

She had fastened pages of *The Highlander* to the wall beside the bed. Instead of a lover's poetry, she began and ended her days with words of radical reform. John Murdoch preached the overthrow of landlords and also gave considerable ink to pointing out the common origins and common miseries of Irish Catholic and Highland Protestant smallholders. Murdoch argued that Scottish crofters should not allow religious bigotry to get in the way of making common cause with—and following the Land League example of—the Irish.

It made sense to Margaret, more sense than what the fundamentalist clergy spewed. Margaret had learned from

Duncan and Annie how to truly listen, hearing the heart within what armors it, hearing the false surety within a tune played too heavy handedly, hearing what speaks more quietly than each day's hunger for bread.

"Maggie?" Calum's voice, Catriona's youngest. "Meeting tonight about Ben Lee. I'm after passing the word."

The lad was gone before Margaret could answer. Ben Lee! Rumor was that the leaseholder was not renewing. The whole of Skye was owned by just ten landlords. Together, MacDonald, MacLeod of Dunvegan, and the proprietors of Glendale and Kilmuir owned about ninety percent of the island. Half the proprietors were absentee landlords. Margaret knew these facts—common knowledge. She also knew that the Valtos and Elishader crofters on the Kilmuir estate—more than 46,000 acres owned by Captain William Fraser, who had bought the land from Lord MacDonald—had gone on rent strike the previous winter.

The Kilmuir crofter petitions for rent reduction had been answered with eviction notices. The crofters' strike, however, had yielded conciliatory response: rents reduced by twenty-five percent, though on the transparent claim by Fraser that a small error had been made in their soumings. Margaret laughed when she heard that.

The carry of a township's common graze was fixed by factor or land surveyor. From the total carry, a proportion, the souming, was allocated each croft, based on wintering capacity or arable land—or on rent paid for it. Management of common graze had become a great source of trouble: overstocking and abuse due to township congestion and limited graze, galling consequences of the clearances.

In determining soumings, one horse equaled eight foals or two cows. One cow equaled eight calves or four stirks, or eight sheep or twelve hogs or sixteen lambs. Ben Lee, with its 3,440 acres, could carry 1200-1400 sheep. It had traditionally been common graze—even Lord MacDonald admitted this. He asserted, however, that since reorganization of the estate early in the century, Ben Lee had been outside officially recognized marches of the Braes township. Thus tenants had used it merely "on sufferance" and had no claim on it and were not entitled to any abatement of rent on its loss.

With due respect to Lord MacDonald, people knew this was havering. In November of 1881, Braes crofters petitioned Lord MacDonald for restoration of Ben Lee. Margaret had signed the paper, as had almost every other Braes tenant. Angus had not been there to say either yea or nay. He had spent the summer fishing out of Kinsale in County Kerry, filling his ears with Irish Land League talk, pouring it into Margaret's ears when he returned, though in a tone more entertained than entrained. She was never sure of his commitments, his sentiments passionately inconsistent.

Trinity spent several days in dazed agitation. She packed and unpacked and half-packed her suitcase, wrote letters to Connell and tore them up, sat hunched on her bed wondering if Connell's cell was bigger than her hostel room, wondered if he thought of her, if he had been disfigured by his injuries, if violence could be just. Trying to encompass bombers and bombed exhausted her. The room became crowded with ancestors and descendants, her dreams full of voices, an implosion of her own silence that carried the shrapnel of the orphaned, starved, transported, dispossessed. The despised and disposed of. To be American; to be beautiful and selfish—the smooth, unbroken skin.

Captain Charles Boycott, former British army officer, was normally a decent man, if foul-tempered and a chronic failure. After abysmal luck at farming, Boycott was hired in 1873 by his avaricious friend, Lord Erne of Lough Mask House in Mayo, to be Erne's estate agent. Erne, an absentee landlord, pressed Boycott to raise tenant rents; then Boycott sacked the estate's laborers over a wage dispute. Eviction notices were served on eleven families. In September of 1881, the parish priest, Father O'Malley, responded by organizing an updated version of an ancient Celtic social weapon—ostracizing.

No one appeared to replace the sacked laborers. The staff deserted. Boycott was shunned. This incensed the captain: he retaliated by denying rent abatements. Eviction processes were obtained, but no one would serve them. Smiths refused to shoe the captain's horses. The baker inexplicably ran out of flour when it came to the captain's bread. The postie delivered only bills to Lough Mask House.

When Boycott's crops ripened, no reapers appeared. Furious, the captain appealed to the northern Orange lodges, and fifty Protestants from Cavan and Monaghan, escorted by 2,000 soldiers, were dispatched south. In Claremorris, fifteen miles from Lough Mask House, not a cart or horse could be found for transport. The Orangemen and their escort had to walk—and it rained. Hard.

Autumn gales followed. The Orangemen and soldiers were encamped on Boycott's lawn and provisioned at his expense. They consumed his pigs, geese, turkeys, ducks, bank account, and self-respect. Some £350 worth of crops were harvested to the tune of £3,500. Boycott left Ireland, his name immortalized by American journalist James Redpath. Any man who rent-racked or who took a farm from which another tenant had been evicted, or who had any traffic with the like, was boycotted.

Legalistic methods were applied by the Land League as well—landlords often losing more at court than would've been gained in rent. League policy was to pay rent on one holding in each district, providing a place for evicted tenants to subsist while remaining in a position to fend off would-be land grabbers. Huts were built, relief work offered, but violence and arrests were frequent, and evicted tenants continued to die on roadsides or disappear on emigrant ships.

Michael Davitt had his ticket of leave from prison revoked and was arrested in February of 1881, serving fifteen grim months in English jails before released again, arriving in Ireland just as Boycott was vacating the country. In October of that busy year, Parnell issued a no-rent manifesto from his cell in Kilmainham prison—in time-honored fashion, the Chief Secretary for Ireland was attempting to control the situation by locking up all the Irish leaders. Under a convenient conspiracy act, each League individual could be held responsible for the utterances and actions of any other League member.

But Davitt flanked this move by endorsing the Ladies' Land League, Ireland's first political association of women, established by Parnell's sister, Anna. Despite clergy outrage, Davitt encouraged women's participation in government affairs. Women Leaguers were arrested and imprisoned but were irrepressible. Resistance increased; money poured in from America; the Land League was declared an illegal organization.

In April of 1881, police opened fire on a crowd blocking process-servers in Count Sligo. Two men fell dead. The crowd reacted, killing the sergeant who gave the order to fire. His men fled.

Fin was arrested that month—though not charged—and lodged in Kilmainham jail, where he heard that Prime Minister Gladstone had introduced a Land Bill for Ireland. Land League secretary Thomas Brennan, in jail with Fin, told him that Parnell supported the bill's acceptance with what amendments as might be possible. Brennan, O'Sullivan, and John Dillon opposed it, but as all three dissenters were in jail, an atmosphere of acceptance conveniently prevailed.

The Gladstone Land Act reeked of compromise. "At least Parnell was cagey," Brennan told Fin. "At the League convention in Dublin he carried a resolution that the Land Act be tested in court by specially selected cases—other tenants waiting to see how those turned out." Brennan shook his head. "A brilliant move. Too bad gutless Ulster tenants fell for the bait of a fucking twenty percent rent reduction."

In October, while Fin still endured confinement, still not charged with any crime, a crowd of women and children gathered at Grawhill. Crown forces fired buckshot into the crowd, then charged with bayonets. Mrs. Mary Deane was cut down by the initial volley; young Ellen McDonagh was stabbed to death. In May of 1882, in Mayo, Parnell's release from prison was cheerfully celebrated by a band of pre-adolescent lads parading with tin whistles and cans. Police met them with buckshot and bayonets. Patrick Melody, running in terror, was killed at his father's feet on the threshold of his home. A day later, Fin and Davitt were both released from prison.

The meeting was packed. Margaret listened to Angus' cousin, Archie MacKinnon, describe what had transpired in Duirnish that February. "John Macpherson called the Glendale meeting, though the landlord had prohibited any gathering of more than three people not in the same family. The penalty for it is eviction and transportation."

Archie paused for the crowd's reflexive shudder. "But Reverend MacRae gave permission for the meeting to be held on church land. John Macpherson told the people at the meeting: no bloodshed. He said we can't plead our just cause if our hands are wet with innocent blood. Those who come against us face-to-face are but vassals of our faceless oppressors."

Donald Patterson shouted from behind Margaret, "What of the innocent blood the brute peelers shed? How much do we bear?"

There was a rumble of agreement: Archie raised his hands for quiet. "The Glendale crofters put cattle and sheep onto land they'd been denied, and deforced the sheriff-officers serving indictments and evictions notices. What was done in Glendale can be done on Ben Lee."

Louder rumbles, Margaret vigorously nodding. The Braes crofters' petition for return of the Ben Lee graze had been rejected by Lord MacDonald's factor. It was time to act. The ache in Margaret's throat was like the hunger that never left her belly. "We must strike," she said, her clear voice floating above the rumbles. "We must take back the land."

Thirty people attended the meeting in Duirnish, Trinity surprised at how many of the faces were familiar to her. Insularity had its cracks. Alie introduced her around. Tea and biscuits were distributed, the mood informal, if resolute. Trinity, the outsider, tried to play the observer, but participation eventually engulfed her. She had skills the community needed. She thought she had been tracking her ancestors these months in Scotland, only to find lineage a circle.

"Can you set up a meeting with Michael Lovat?" she asked Alie on the drive home. "And gather the written material that's pertinent to the proposal?"

"Certainly."

"And find me a handbook on grant writing?"

"Aye."

"Anything else?"

"Come to the ceilidh Friday. You'll like it."

Trinity hunched her shoulders. The windshield wipers rubbed stoically back and forth, the rain undaunted. Night, rain, dashboard glow; the piper's hands easy on the wheel. Trinity felt heated by his masculinity, felt the danger of trusting the interiorness of the moment. At journey's end would be the rude blast of wind, slash of rain when the car door opened, warmth and intimacy fled. She would be on her own again, ashes in the hearth.

Alie turned his head at her silence. "Still here?"

"Umm."

THE SELKIE'S LINEAGE

He downshifted, rounded the tight bend out of Staffin, climbing above the coast, wipers striving to make the world distinct. "What's eating you?"

Trinity tucked her arms across her waist. "Unfinished business." Centuries of it.

Alie glanced at her, topping the hill at Glasphein. "Want to talk about it? Might help."

She shook her head, silence the only reliable continuity, even damaged as it had become. They went on, the one-lane blacktop threading between crofts, past quiet Digg, Dùnan, the dark privacy of mist and rain.

"There's a story in my mother's family," the piper said, "of how one of my ancestors came by his gift of music." He flicked the heater control higher, as if adding a peat to the fire. Trinity said nothing.

"In Loch Maree there's an island, Sitheanan Dubha, said to be a fairy place, with a well of healing waters on it. My ancestor, Iain MacKenzie by name, fished the loch. His brother, Duncan, in Kinlochewe, was a weaver and a brilliant bard, but Iain was more ordinary. The whole family was poorer than you can imagine—hard times with the clearances, the old way of life unraveling.

"One night—cold and wet like this, but autumn instead of summer, and fair more of a wind—Iain's wee girl fell sick and couldn't be helped. Iain took the boat over the loch to fetch a doctor, though too poor to pay, of course; he would've offered service in kind."

They were nearing Flodigarry, Alie driving slowly, with a calmness Trinity was beginning to see beyond.

"Iain's boat swamped in rough waves, and he somehow washed up on the shore of the fairy isle, stranded there until rescued next day by men sent searching by Iain's wife. The child had died. Traveled on, as they used to say.

"It was after that night that Iain became a piper, one of the finest of his time. But he wouldn't speak of his night on Sitheanan Dubha, except once to his wife and his brother,

Duncan. His wife asked Iain if his piping gift from the fairies had been bought with his daughter's life, choiceless or not."

Alie turned into the hostel driveway, coasted down the hill and pulled up beside the door, putting the car into neutral. "Iain replied that there is no bargaining—only resolve and acceptance. The two became one on Sitheanan Dubha."

The Braes community was bordered by Loch Sligachan on the south, by the Sound of Raasay on the east, by Ben Lee on the west; it could only be reached along a winding track running south from Portree. Angus Martin, officer in charge of serving notices in Braes, clerk to the factor, traveled that track on April 7, 1882, with his assistants, Ewan Robertson and Norman Beaton. The clerk carried removal summonses to be delivered to the rebellious townships: Lord MacDonald's response to crofter defiance. The thrawn fools insisted on putting stock on Ben Lee and moreover refused to pay their rents. Dozens of eviction notices were in Martin's pockets: it would be a long day.

Martin expected to be greeted with dismay, even contrition—the crofters were, after all, religious folk. Instead, when Martin and his assistants reached Gedintailor, they were met by an angry, obdurate crowd, mostly female.

"Five hundred at least," whispered Robertson.

"Ach, no, man. No more than a hundred or so," scoffed Beaton.

Martin attempted stern assertion of legal mission.

At his words Mairi nic Fhuilaidh cried out, "Make them burn the summonses!"

Iain Nicolson yelled to the servers, "Put the papers down on the road!"

Martin did so, hands trembling, making a heap of papers, acutely aware of the implacable stones weighing dozens of tenant hands. Young Calum came trotting through the crowd carrying a burning peat, so serious and wild that he never saw Margaret as he passed her. Martin, Beaton, and Robertson watched the papers burn—the crowd silent, then jeering, as the officers turned back toward Portree.

Ten days after, at six in the morning, two sheriffs, two fiscals, a police captain, forty-seven Glasgow policemen, and ten county constables retraced the process-servers' journey, carrying warrants for the arrest of five of the Braes deforcers.

Child sentries in the hills overlooking the Portree track sounded warning. Once again, a crowd hastily gathered. As before, it was predominantly female—most of the men away in Ireland at the fishing. The hundred who gathered in bleak incessant rain were not well-prepared for confrontation. The summons had shaken them from their beds; they arrived disheveled and anxious.

Sheriff Ivory, eager to crush the budding agitation movement, took advantage, making his arrests, but the crowd grew. Stones and mud began to fly. Police dropped to the ground, injured; others charged, swinging batons. But the women held position, the formidable Marion MacMillan in the fore. Margaret saw the prisoners herded away from the action and saw her neighbor, Effie Stewart, a fisherman's widow, shriek and fall bleeding from a head wound. Fleet as any lad, Margaret turned and ran for the brow of the hill.

The road was cut along the face of a steep declivity rising sheer to a height of four hundred feet. The place was called An Cumhang, and the crofters had heaped boulders atop the hill. Margaret was closely tailed by Calum and other tenants as the battle broke off, police hustling up the road with their injured and prisoners. It was a race.

"Push! Push!" Margaret panted, as the first boulders began grinding, then hurtling to the road below. There were screams—stone finding flesh—but the police won through to open ground. Furious crofters closed with them in hand-to-hand combat—police now using rocks as well as batons. The women were ferocious fighters but were eventually forced to withdraw from open country, bloodied, unrecalcitrant. No more the bended head.

Parnell subsumed the Land League, using it to power his Home Rule movement. He had not wanted to dilute fenianism with agrarian reform: converting peasants into proprietors turned them into conservatives. Davitt's socialism was tolerated—his integrity unquestionable—but his land nationalization cause was not embraced. Parnell pointedly, though unmaliciously, spoke against it. With the so-called Kilmainham Treaty agreed to by the jailed Parnell in the spring of 1882, the Land War in Ireland essentially ended. Davitt and O'Sullivan, finally released from Portland prison, their latest incarceration, were met by Parnell and escorted to London.

"You've thrown it away," Davitt said in the car, sitting in back with Parnell and Dillon, O'Sullivan and O'Kelly in front. "The treaty is a disaster, nothing but political opportunism. You're no revolutionary, Charles."

"I'm aware of your feelings on this, Michael," Parnell returned without heat. "But look at the crimes and outrages perpetrated during my imprisonment. And have you any idea of the money spent by the Ladies' League? It was imperative we slow the agitation."

"It was the ladies who broke Secretary Forster—negating the coercion—and got us all, you included, out of jail," Davitt said quietly. "Funds well spent, I'd say."

"I was told the MPs in Commons roared and cheered when it was announced you were back in prison," Fin said to Davitt. "But we're not finished yet."

Parnell raised his brows. "Home rule must be our focus. I would think a committed fenian like yourself would see that, Fin."

"Ah, man, but I do. Selling out the Land League sold out those same people you're wanting to free. But then, I'm just a fucking peasant, Charles."

That night, word came from Dublin that Lord Cavendish had been murdered in Phoenix Park by a group styling themselves The Invincibles. Parnell collapsed, then tried unsuccessfully to resign from Parliament. When the Arrears Act passed, offering conciliatory terms, Parnell more than ever was determined to put the brakes on reform agitation; he refused funding to the Ladies' Land League. But at that same time, during three days in one district alone, 150 families—750 persons—were evicted for arrears dating from famine years.

Parnell replaced the Land League with a National League. Local self-government, home rule, and parliamentary and municipal reform were the new league's aims. Land reform was in the platform as well, but under Parnell's control. He had become too vulnerable. The Phoenix Park killing led to a Crimes Bill: secret courts of inquiry, suppression of newspapers, banning of meetings, abolishing of jury trials in many cases. Secretary Forster intended to implicate Parnell in the Phoenix Park tragedy—for not using his influence to prevent it.

Parnell scorned to defend himself against English opinion: his power came from the Irish; his accountability was to the Irish. In 1882 Davitt was elected to Parliament, then disqualified by a special vote of the House of Commons because he was a treason-felony prisoner on a ticket of leave.

1882 was another poor season for Highland potatoes. But crofters continued to agitate. Sympathizers paid the fines levied on the Braes deforcers. In September, court orders were served on fifty-three Braes tenants, but the messengers were pelted with stones, forcing their retreat. Sheriff Ivory and his sheriff-substitutes had their request for military intervention turned down; they added fifty constables to their ranks. In October, tenants prevented this force from entering Braes. Then the Kilmuir tenants in the north of Skye began a new rent strike.

A great storm pounded the Highlands in October, destroying over 1,200 boats with all their nets and gear, devastating crops. December heightened the reality of scarcity as severe winter weather ripped through the isles, the worst winter since the 1840s. Margaret and her neighbors sold breeding stock in order to buy meal. The government did nothing.

Calum and his sister, Mairi, sat at Margaret's hearth, eating thin porridge: never enough food, but it was of land hunger they talked. "In the newest *Highlander*," Margaret said, scraping the last of the porridge into Mairi's bowl, "Reverend Donald MacCallum writes of land being our birthright—as the air and sunlight and water are our birthrights."

Calum nodded, resonant with this elemental verity.

"Here on Skye, Alexander MacDonald manages five estates. Did you know that? Five! Archie says this means he holds sway over more than eight of every ten of us on this island. Besides which, he's Skye's only lawyer, our tax collector, and captain of the Portree Volunteers. Also bank agent and on the school boards of six parishes."

"And raises the rents of any tenant doesn't touch his cap when he sees him," added Calum.

"But we're not going to give in." Mairi licked her horn spoon like a cat; a fastidious girl of sixteen whose hunger made her obsessively intent on details. Soon, like her older sister, she would be going to Inverness to work as a servant.

"Indeed not," Margaret agreed. "Only this month Lord MacDonald promised us Ben Lee—for an atrocious rent— but it shows that the lairds are taking us seriously at last. I read in *The Highlander* that Sir William Harcourt has suggested a Royal Commission look into our grievances."

"A Royal Commission to come here?" asked Mairi. "To Skye?"

"To Braes, even," said Margaret. "Aye, to us."

Hogmanay came and went. In February, John Murdoch reported the founding of the Highland Land Law Reform Association with its program of mass rent strikes, demonstrations, and resistance to police and military force. The stated aim of the HLLRA was, *To obtain for the Highland people the right to live on their native soil under equitable conditions.* Margaret quickened to these words, read in the gloom of her blackhouse, lightly stroking one child-boned finger under the line of print as if tracing a map of the Gaels' journey.

Fin O'Sullivan, sent by Davitt, attended the HLLRA meeting with D. H. MacFarlane, a converted Catholic whom Fin had met as a Parnellite MP from Carlow, before MacFarlane's return to his native Highlands. Fin said little at the meeting but was pleased with the selection of MacFarlane as president of the fledgling reform organization, though he knew many Highlanders mistrusted MacFarlane's Catholicism.

John Murdoch, whom Fin had also known in Ireland, shared his regard for MacFarlane. "The smallholders' plight is the same, Ireland or Scotland," Murdoch said to Fin. "Though in Ireland, rent's the thing, and here, land itself is the issue."

"Parnell fetters the league in Ireland," said Fin. "His politicking—and Kitty O'Shea—have unmanned him. The Kilmainham Treat is unabidable."

"I fear for him."

"And well you should."

Angus came home in March, weary, wind-scoured, marginally richer for months of dangerous winter fishing out of Lewis. "Dirty weather," he said of it, and Margaret did not dwell on Gairloch memories. She waited on her husband as Highland women did their men. Little enough to give; women gave it, though not always soft-handedly.

Margaret set out bannocks and butter and a bowl of cream with dried oatmeal on top. She lit the crusie lamp with its white bulrush looped in the iron saucer of fish oil, the wick's end leaning against the shallow, spouted rim. She took up her knitting, clever fingers quick as wrens, habit closer than thought.

Angus ate, then smoked, looking at his wife from time-to-time. "Wild as a tink, I hear you are," he said when she carried over his whisky and returned to her knitting.

"Wheest, what rubbish, this?"

"A wonder I don't come home and find you in jail."

"The strikes? Is that what you're on about?"

"Strikes and warring with the police, aye, and speaking up at meetings like some limmer in breeks."

Margaret's astonishment brought a cessation to her knitting. Angus tossed back his whisky, then rose, putting on hat and coat, striding out.

Fin sat on the long-bench in Hugh MacRae's cottage in Glendale, listening to the thrash of rain and the cow's rustle in the next room, as she stirred the bracken bedding with slow restlessness. Hugh and his neighbor, Neil MacLeod, and Neil's brother, Murdo, had been arrested and fined in the latest deforcement. "Though it was the women did the dirty work," Hugh admitted to Fin, handing him a whisky. "They like to've stoned those brutes."

Catherine MacRae grimly smiled from her spinning wheel; her daughter, Janet, flicked a glance at Fin from where she perched on the edge of the boxbed, knitting, rocking her sister's cradle with a nudging foot.

Fin sipped his whiskey. His gut hurt as it had ever since the bayonet wound; the whisky's warmth eased it. He tuned out the ache—and the girl's glances. This March trip was his second to the Highlands. The landscape reminded him of Donegal, though the Highlands now largely lacked the social music still common in Ireland. More's the pity, Fin thought. Lasses better off doing their flirting at the ceilidh house than under dour talk at their parents' tables.

Fin early found that Highland crofters needed no outside agitator to spur them. He had traveled to branch league meetings with Glendale's John Macpherson, a broad-shouldered, thundering orator. Macpherson had intelligence, conviction, and wit. He was an easy man to respect, though Fin, used to Davitt's utter selflessness—and the cynical, brutal edge found in fenians too many generations into unsuccessful, sometimes ludicrous guerilla rebellion—thought Macpherson naïve, if embroiled.

The Glendale blackhouse in which Fin sat could easily be an Irishman's hut; the Highland peat fire in the hearth an Irish turf fire. But the girl and her hungry Protestant glances—no, nothing of him could feed such as her. Fin had paced human desire out of himself during his prison terms, indeterminate terms when he may as well have been sealed in a wall, his blood the prison's mortar. Freed, a relative condition, Fin both cherished and shunned such things as music, dance, courtship, the light of a smile, the curve of a breast.

The door of the Kilmuir village hall was propped open with the same robust stone that usually held it shut. Up the road from the hall, Flora MacDonald's monument stretched its slender stone neck in the twilight; a ways beyond, the broken walls of Duntulm Castle listened to an old and constant wind. In the hall itself was light, music, laughter, the stomp of dancing feet, the glint of bottles, the smoke of many cigarettes, the surf of banter in English and Gaelic.

For Trinity, coming to this ceilidh was unlike attending similar occasions with Connell. The single-minded sexuality of their coupleness—as close to courtship as Connell ever came—and his indifference to social context, was absent for her here. Trinity whirled in a strip-the-willow, passed from hand-to-hand like a flurry of gossip. On the low stage, Alie played whistle; Fiona Martin was a dervish on the fiddle; her sister, Eilidh, denimed knees braced wide, maneuvered a squeezebox; and Big Paddy from Uig flailed his guitar. Thanks to Alie, Trinity knew them all.

Several jigs and reels later, the band leaned back into a waltz. Alie put aside his whistle, heading for Trinity, but Chris Docherty reached her first and swung her into the dance's eddies, ignoring her reluctance. "Is it Irishmen you're chary of, or linesmen, perhaps? Or is it just me you don't like?"

"Socially skittish, is all. Nothing personal," Trinity said into his heavy shoulder. Her reclusiveness had become a social crime now that it had a social context.

"How long did you know Connell O'Sullivan?" Chris asked. They rounded a corner, bumping into a dawdling couple.

"Not long. An abbreviated affair. You?"

Chris steered her toward the door. "Come outside for a breather. I've a bottle in Calum's car."

"Outside sounds fine; the car too far."

He dropped his palm from her waist but kept hold of her hand, leading her through the crowd in the foyer and a second crowd outside the door. Though late, it was not wholly dark; instead, a deep indigo, star-pricked. The breeze had a welcome sea bite. Trinity leaned on the stone wall beside the hall, body damp with sweat, a trickle of it between her breasts.

Chris lit a cigarette. "You knew Connell well enough to develop an ear for Belfast accents," he said, pocketing his lighter.

"A writer's ear."

Chris drew on the cigarette, not looking at her. The smell of tobacco enveloped them, whipped away by the breeze.

"The subject pains me," Trinity said after a while.

Chris shifted, straightened from the wall. "I can see that."

"Then why push? Where's your famous Celtic subtlety?"

He scratched his chin with the hand holding the cigarette, then took another drag. Trinity was beginning to chill in the breeze.

"I don't know," he said. "It just seems there's no getting in the door with you until that obstacle's out of the way. A dead relationship, isn't it?" He tossed the cigarette butt into the road, a scatter of sparks. Trinity thought of bombs.

"It was you resurrected it, telling me he's alive."

"In prison."

"How long a sentence?"

"Eleven years."

She couldn't absorb this thought. Connell's tread endlessly pacing the cage of her consciousness. "Were you his friend?"

"I knew him."

"That's not what I asked."

Chris shrugged. "You're not the only one with subjects to avoid." He nodded toward the hall door. "Someone looking for you, I believe."

Alie had spotted them but did not approach. Trinity pushed away from the wall. "I'm cold."

"Ye needn't tell me twice," Chris muttered.

Lord Napier stroked one finger along his chin as he listened to John Mathieson offer testimony to the Royal Commission. Braes was the commission's first session. The lord glanced at his fellow appointees: MacKenzie of Gairloch, Cameron of Lochiel, Fraser MacIntosh, Professor

MacKinnon, and Sheriff Nicolson. Napier himself was a Highland landlord who had cleared his estates. But the elite had weakened; policies needed to be revised; public opinion's tide had turned. So here they sat meticulously questioning crofters about the grievances of people who lived like animals, from the looks of what passed for homes. Even in May's lamb-frisking sunlight, the blackhouses appalled Napier.

It had been explained to the lords that croft houses were made by building two drystone dykes, one within the other, and filling the gaps with earth and rubble. The walls were six or seven feet high with a slight taper at the top. Rafters were improvised out of such things as driftwood, old oars, and masts, covered with turf and thatch—secured with heather ropes weighted with stones. There were no eaves.

The shape was long and low, the roof rounded, the floor earthen. Better dwellings had two doors, two small windows, and flooring; perhaps two rooms. Older blackhouses had no windows or chimney. Furnishings were planks, barrels, stools, and a roofed boxbed. Crofters lived at one end of the house, beasts at the other; chickens lodged in the rafters.

During testimony the commissioners were told, "The crofters cannot do without heather ropes, in order to fasten the thatch upon the house. There is one day set apart by the gamekeeper upon which you are allowed to go and pull heather to make ropes. You cannot attend on another day or you are liable to be fined for it."

When the commissioners traveled to Glendale, John Macpherson told the lords, "We are frugal and not extravagant in our way of living, our staple food being meal, potatoes, and fish—when it is got. We have very miserable dwelling houses and never get aid from our proprietors to build better ones; they are thatched with straw, and, as our crofts do not produce the required amount of straw necessary for fodder for the cattle and thatch for the houses, and, as we are prohibited by the proprietor from cutting rushes or heather, the condition of our dwelling houses in rainy weather is most deplorable. Of the twenty crofters' houses in the township, there are only two in which the cattle are not under the same roof with the family. Now, we leave it to your lordships to see what this revelation of the condition of our dwellings reflects on the boasted civilization of the nineteenth century."

Napier listened. The commission doggedly went from township to township through spring, summer, and fall, into the winter of that year, taking testimony, asking tireless detailed questions. Alexander MacKenzie and *The Highlander's* John Murdoch also toured the area, providing advice and trying to ensure that crofters who testified remained immune from intimidation or reprisal. During this time, district branches of the Land League were formed and pamphlets printed in English and Gaelic.

It was eye opening for Lord Napier. He subsequently wrote of the crofters: *His habitation is usually of a character which would almost imply physical and moral degradation in the eyes of those who do not know how much decency, courtesy, virtue, and even mental refinement survive amidst the sordid surroundings of a Highland hovel.*

In August, while the Napier Commission was in session, Fin traveled to Fraserburgh, where a mass meeting of the west coast herring fishermen was taking place. Fin had been back to Ireland, over to London, and again to the Highlands since spring. Fatigue he considered irrelevant, likewise the increasing yearning for a home life. Lacking experience of such, the yearning—if identified at all in his mind—was diagnosed as sexual angst and suppressed. Fin's entire existence had been dedicated to ceaseless uphill struggle: to survive, to free Ireland, to endure and transcend prison. To fulfill ancestral obligations stainlessly, with a warrior's self-sacrifice, a peasant's—a king's—brute tenacity.

In Fraserburgh, Fin left his lodgings early in the morning, cat-tense reflexes unable to relent into the peace of deep, vulnerable sleep. Fatigue fed into itself, a simultaneous drain and demand that held him in perpetual deprivation. He functioned in defiance of it as he had survived the poorhouse in defiance of reasonable expectation. Authority would not own him; the English would not govern him; evil would not defeat him; not even his own body would control him.

Reaching the waterfront, Fin walked past the boats newly drawn up from the night's fishing, their nets spread to dry, their smell of tar and bilge and herring. The curing station's bustle drew him: teams of women and girls beheading, gutting, sorting, and packing thousands of shimmering, fresh-caught herring. The women stood in the raw morning, their knives flashing. Forty fish a minute skimmed through each gutter's calico-bandaged hands. The seamlessly fast, repetitious movements were hypnotic. Fin moved closer, only half-hearing the women's banter, the sly remarks in east coast Doric and west coast Gaelic.

One woman, small and lithe, dressed like the others but with hair that came past her hips in a half-braided twisting flow, worked without speaking, ignoring Fin's presence. He discovered himself wanting her attention, not to make an impression but in a sudden unconsidered need to be within this woman's world, whatever it might be. Plainly, it was not the world the other women, or Fin himself, crudely occupied.

"Gawk at that one all ye like, yer wastin' yer time," one of the local women advised, passing near him. "She hasnae voice—nor ony interest in bit men." The packer leered, bumping Fin with her hip. "Why not try yer luck wi' someone mair couthy?"

Fin shook his head, moving aside, continuing to wonder at the silent dimension in which the woman moved, as though in depths so sensitive to intention's conception that words would be gross intrusion. Still, words were what Fin had. He tarried, exhausting the other women of ribald suggestions and earnest efforts to divert his interest.

"My name is Fin O'Sullivan," he said, finally stepping forward. "Will you come walk with me later?"

She shook her head without looking up.

Next morning, he was back. He'd attended the fishermen's meeting, a massive, energetic affair that would lead to the formation of branch Land League associations in various widespread Highland areas once the fishermen returned home. It would be a tremendous enlargement of agitation, and Fin was pleased. But his private energies had narrowed in fixation on the unspeaking herring gutter.

The women smirked and catcalled when Fin arrived. Fishermen looked sidelong at him. Fin settled near the mute woman's workstation, shared with two other women. Knives flashed, hands blurred, fish shimmered and were reduced to mundane products. Misty damp hung in the air like the reproachful ghosts of a million dead herring. The women's long skirts were heavy with it. Each gutter's left hand was scarred from the unforgiving knives: their penance. The men who fished carried their own fell marks. It was more an army than a work force; and successful boat skippers were as legendary as generals.

Fin stayed almost two hours that day. The women were impressed at this vigil despite their pique at his lack of response to them. "What is her name?" he asked a stolid, sensible looking gutter at an adjacent station.

"No one knows," she said without pausing in her work; fish entrails flicked past him. "She's a stranger to all of us. No one kens her."

Fin approached the mute woman. "Lass," he said, though her age was unguessable. "Will you come out for a walk with me? A simple walk is all I'm asking—a walk, a meal, whatever you like."

She shook her head, the slight motion absolute negation.

The third day, Fin was there again, but came when the work was nearly done. The women chided him for tardiness. Their fondness for him had grown; it was unfamiliar to Fin, aloof from relationships, his sisters and mother long vanished, detached from community by his lifestyle—and prison.

When the last herring went from her hands into the appropriate barrel, Fin came to her and said, "Fionaghalla."

She looked up sharply. Her eyes were lavender-grey and her gaze was watchful. Fin encountered no sense of soul in that gaze, only color, depth, awareness offering no revelation of relationship with other. Without thinking, he crossed himself.

She looked down, turned away, removing her oiled apron.

Fin rallied. "Fionaghalla?" Her name in his Celtic mind.

She finished cleaning her knife, stowed it.

A third time: "Fionaghalla, come with me to Ireland."

Her gaze was on him again.

Her soul is in a shell in her pocket, he thought.

She buttoned her close-fitting jacket and walked with him away from the beach.

The Napier Commission's report was published in 1884. It was criticized by the spectrum's extremes—estate owners and landless cottars—but was a symbolic victory for the crofters; an affirmation of their plight. They continued defying landlords by grazing stock in forbidden areas. Chief Constable McHardy on Skye reported these rebellions to the Home Office, which replied by sending fifty revolvers and ammunition to arm Skye's police. The law force was increased to twelve constables at each station in the Uig and unruly Kilmuir districts.

The House of Commons was informed by the Home Secretary that, "The conduct of these Skye crofters can no longer be tolerated." In October, three gunboats were dispatched. The crew of the chartered *Lochiel* refused to sail her on this mission against the islanders; they were sacked and blacklisted by MacBraynes, who owned her, and replaced with a special crew recruited from the south. Forty armed police and five or six hundred marines were aboard the *Lochiel*. They were joined in Portree by the gunboat *Assistance* with three hundred fifty marines and one hundred blue jackets, and the *Bantever* with sixty-five more marines. The crofters maintained passive resistance, sharing food and drink with the marines but refusing to pay rents, withdraw stock, or observe interdicts. John Macpherson calmly explained this policy to Sheriff Ivory, who fumed.

Meanwhile, the crofters dug potatoes in every township along Skye's coast, ignoring the presence of the gunboats. *The Glasgow Herald* reported, "The results of the threatened expedition to the country of the crofters must be described, so far, as totally unsatisfactory." Expeditions also failed at Uig, Staffin, and Kilmuir to the island's north.

Sheriff Ivory resolved to "storm Glendale by sea and land." Ivory and the chief constable, fiscal, and lieutenant colonel led twenty police and three companies of marines with artillery ashore at Colbost jetty and marched to Hamara Lodge in Glendale. Cresting the hill from Colbost, they came on a Land League meeting just as Free Church Elder John MacKay was closing with a prayer in Gaelic.

Marine buglers attempted to disrupt the gathering, but the six hundred crofters coolly finished their business and dispersed. The marines continued to the lodge, which was garrisoned with six police, seventy-five marines, and three thousand rounds of ammunition. For all this provocative display of force, the invasion flopped; crofters remained self-disciplined, decorous, and unintimidated.

Trinity's meeting with Michael Lovat, the solicitor from Fort William, was elucidating. She prepared by immersing in the written material Alie had brought to the hostel in an empty Talisker carton, taking notes as the piper outlined the community's vision regarding the Ferinurchar estate. Keeping her relationship with Alie businesslike was difficult.

"What's wrong with a little romance?" Alie asked.

"Nothing," Trinity said, doodling sheep in the margin of her notes. "You're polite not to instead ask what's wrong with me."

Alie smiled—always the gentler path. "Did you enjoy the ceilidh?"

"Sure. It was fun."

"What changed your mind about going? Decided you're keen on the Irishman after all?"

Trinity shook her head, still doodling. "Morag. I went with her and her sister-in-law."

"I see she has more influence than I do."

Trinity shrugged. "She's decided I brood too much."

"She's right. Melancholy doesn't suit you. Maybe you should go dancing more often."

"Yes, well…."

Michael Lovat met Trinity at the Cuillin Hills Hotel in Portree, there on other business. They drank tea as they talked, sitting by a wide window looking out over Portree's postcard harbor and beyond to the unflinching dignity of the Cuillin. An expensive view once you entered the hotel; the adamant line drawn by a pane of glass.

Lovat was a midforties, rakishly attractive man with the kind of fact-filing mind also found in successful politicians. He treated Trinity with a politeness marking him faithfully married, warming to her only when she showed some understanding of the land issue's complex roots.

THE SELKIE'S LINEAGE

"I confess I was dubious when Alie told me he'd gotten an American to write the funding proposals," Lovat said, pouring more tea in an impatiently meticulous way.

"I'm still dubious," Trinity said, stirring in milk, wiping a spattered drop from her open notebook. "So, instruct me."

At the hostel afterward, she changed from slacks to jeans, from tweed jacket to sweatshirt and began organizing her notes on the dining room table. She worked steadily until dusk, when Alie appeared, bog-stained from his job with the crew laying a new waterline from Storr Lochs to Portree.

"Haven't you been home yet?" Trinity asked.

"Hoping to seduce you with my manly grime," he said, wiping a shirtsleeve across his nose. "Actually, I was dropping off a hosteler I picked up hitchhiking at Lealt. Thought I'd see how your meeting with Michael went."

"Very informative. He's an interesting man."

"Married. Did he tell you?"

"In his own wee way." She leafed through a stack of file cards. "There are a bunch of things I need you to clarify. Got a minute?"

"I have all night." He glanced around the hostel dining room, guests congregating for meal preparation. "It's noisy here. Why don't you come over to my place? I'll provide dinner—after I shower, of course—and you can ask your questions."

Trinity surveyed the room's escalating activity and began gathering up her papers.

Alie's place was a whitewashed cottage, small but clean other than the untidiness of the day. "Help yourself to coffee or tea," he told her, switching on the electric kettle. " I'll go make myself delectable."

Trinity drifted around the room while he showered. There were three small rooms, bedroom and bathroom, she assumed, down the short hall. She sat on the pot-holed taupe sofa; Alie's pipes were heaped on the coffee table. Various sized whistles lay in open cases on the floor.

"Do you burn peat?" Trinity asked when the piper emerged, hair towel-rumpled, in clean jeans and a SKAT T-shirt.

"Coal, modern man that I am."

Dinner was a boldly spiced mousaka, Alie having turned to cooking with the same absorption he'd given whisky and music.

"Fantastic," Trinity said, herself a lax cook, particularly since coming to Scotland, living in hostels.

"I wasn't much use in the kitchen until after my wife left me."

"Your cooking was that bad?"

"She fell in love with someone else."

"Oh." Trinity backed off the subject. They finished eating and moved to the sofa, spending an hour going through Trinity's list of questions for the Ferinurchar grant. The sensuous wail of a Davy Spillane CD played in the background. "Can you play uillean pipes?"

"Never tried. I was brought up on pibroch and pipe bands." He reached over to stroke her hand with one finger, as though calming a budgie. She looked at him, and the finger stilled. "I wonder who you really are inside the tamper-proof lid. Is anyone there?"

"Am I so insubstantial? Chris calls me the ghost."

"I don't know what you are. A fantasy projection?"

"Is fantasy what you're after?"

"Mystery, maybe?" He leaned, in classic style, to kiss her, questing.

Trinity drew away. "I can't do this."

Alie tightened, curbed, then let her go, not one to insist, no pelt with which to bargain.

In 1885, D. H. MacFarlane won the Argyll seat as the crofters' candidate. In 1886, the Crofters' Holding Act was passed, granting hereditary security of tenure and fair and reasonable rents to tenants. It also—as a sop to landlords, to prevent their cheap labor pool from gaining economic independence—limited croft size. The Crofters' Act was a landmark measure, but ignored the reality of the cottars and did not restore land already lost. Land raids continued, agitation even intensified, and a military presence was maintained on Skye until 1888.

In the spring of 1887, Michael Davitt, with Fin in his retinue, came to the Highlands on the invitation of the crofters. The hall in Wick, where they began their tour, was suffocatingly crowded. From Wick they journeyed south through Sutherland and Easter Ross, welcomed everywhere.

At Bonar Bridge, Davitt's carriage was enthusiastically dragged through the streets by Land Leaguers who unyoked the horses. Much the same scene occurred at Dingwall. At Strome, the open-air rally was attended by hundreds of crofters and fishermen.

Davitt told the cheering crowd, "In traveling down the lovely glens which stretch from here to Dingwall, I could not help feeling the blood boil within me when hearing of how the people have been cleared away to make room for sheep or for hunting grounds for landlord-sportsmen. When seeing on every side the evidence of what Nature has done to make these valleys so fitted to be the abode of an industrious and happy population, and when recollecting, on the other hand, how all those blessings of Nature are denied to the people through an inhuman landlordism, I have felt more strongly than ever the link of sympathy which binds me to the Celtic race of the Highlands. The exterminator's hand which has depopulated Ireland has also been busy with destruction here."

He pressed the crofters not to be content with security of tenure but to work for the return of land lost during the clearances and for eradication of landlordism itself.

On Saturday, May seventh, Margaret woke early, stirred by the prospect of seeing the great Irishman, Michael Davitt, in Portree that evening. Angus, beside her in the boxbed, heavily slept; Margaret rose and dressed, then went outside. The morning was fresh and brilliant, as May in the Hebrides is wont to be. Light lay over the land. Margaret was thirty-seven; Angus fifty. But it seemed, standing in the Braes dawn with her arms folded under her breasts, breeze ruffling her uncombed hair, that she was nothing but the lass she'd always been—Margaret Ross, daughter of a brave man and brave woman who taught her that courage and loyalty and love are paramount and inseparable.

An old longing swept over her for the sound of her father's fiddle and for the sight of him: his easy stance, his tapping foot; and Annie's quick, affectionate glance at him over her knitting. Margaret had yet to meet a better man than Duncan, though she thought Michael Davitt might come close.

By afternoon, the sky open-mindedly allowed a few clouds to stray in, but it was still fine weather for the trip to Portree. Margaret went with Angus and Archie, and Archie's wife, Morag, their two grown children, and Donald and Catriona; young Calum was along with his wife and new bairn; a crowd to join other crowds converging on Portree's pier.

There was wild excitement when Davitt stepped ashore from the Strome steamer, Fin and the others behind him. Davitt was swept to the front of what became a cheering procession led by a piper up the hill to Wentworth Street and on to Davitt's lodgings at the Portree Hotel. Margaret was jostled from every side as she stood in the crush at Somerled Square, thousands of Skye folk unwilling to leave without a few words from this modest Irish hero.

The crowd's continuous shouting at last compelled Davitt's appearance at one of the hotel's upper windows.

Tall, dark, with Fin a cool shadow behind him, he spoke to the throng: "I thank you from the bottom of my heart for the warmth with which you've received me. I know that the sympathy you have shown by this enthusiastic welcome is extended more to the people I represent than to myself on account of anything that I have done personally."

Three days later, Davitt spoke at a huge demonstration in Portree, but Margaret did not attend. That morning she received a letter from her sister-in-law in Nova Scotia. It was the first time Johanna had ever written—the only news from David and his wife since before Duncan's death. Margaret took the letter outside to read it in the light.

Dear Maggie,
I am sorry to be writing this sad news but knew you would want to know. Our Murdoch was lost at sea along with all the crew of the Osprey. Some of their gear was found in the water by other fishermen, but no bodies.
We are heartbroken, though Murdoch left us for the fishing life at seventeen, and we hardly saw him after. He married a fine Cape Breton girl, Meredith MacIssac, two years ago, who's now expecting.
If it's any comfort, Murdoch always remembered you even though you parted when he was only three. He grew up well-liked by everyone—never a complainer or vain—and had his own way about him, those calm, grey eyes and flashing smile. And he could always find the fish.
I hope you know I loved him even if he wasn't mine.
Faithfully,
Johanna Ross

Margaret carefully folded the letter and tucked it into her jacket sleeve. She rose from the bench beside the cottage and walked stiffly away, a heaviness upon her as though the years had become stones. She climbed the ridge above the fank, onto reclaimed grazing land, hard-fought. Everything in their lives hard-fought except loss: that came sudden and easy, like slipping on a kelpy rock at low tide.

Thirty years old, he would be.

Margaret climbed Ben Lee with its smooth, green grass and grey couthy stones. She walked and did not sit or rest because stillness could not be borne. It was like it had been after Duncan.

When she came down to the cottage again, it was afternoon, and Angus had gone with the others to the rally in Portree. She took her father's fiddle from the kist in which it was kept, and held it on her lap.

Late that night when Angus came in—more than a little drunk, refreshment taken in the company of Davitt's compatriot, Fin O'Sullivan—she told him she had been thinking to send the fiddle to Murdoch's wife, for the bairn, but feared it would not survive intact. "So I'm taking it to her myself, for Murdoch's son, as I think it will be."

"Taking it to Canada? Have you gone skite, woman? What rubbish!"

Margaret said nothing, but Angus could tell she would not change her mind.

"If you go, you'll not be coming back into any house of mine."

"I will," Margaret said. "Never doubt it."

Their Highland tour completed, Fin returned with Davitt to Dublin. Michael had met Mary Yore on a lecture tour the previous year and married her, honeymooning in America and coming to live in a thrifty Dublin house given them by Land League friends. The house was the only gift Davitt ever accepted from the League.

Believing that Irish independence could only be won with the support of the British working class, Davitt was becoming more and more involved in the Labor movement and in advocating industrial safety, worker's compensation, and worker's pensions. He wanted an alliance with the British working class as he had with Highland crofters, though emphatically wanted Irish trade unions to be free of British control.

The Irish Land League having been replaced with Parnell's National League, Fin was spending less time with Davitt and more time in IRB activities, though his admiration for the one leader whose integrity Fin never saw compromised remained lifelong. There was little satisfaction to be got from the IRB's limited actions, but Fin had no faith in the labyrinth course Parnell steered in Parliament. 1885 had challenged Parnell's powers to the utmost, and, if he triumphed, Fin still knew the man's weaknesses; Parnell, unlike Davitt, was not of one piece.

The turmoil in the early '80s returned with the passage of a new Land Act allowing revising of the judicial rents fixed under the '81 act. The new '87 land bill was preceded by a stringent Coercion Bill that meant National League meeting rooms could be searched, documents confiscated, newspapers suppressed, and political prisoners be treated like ordinary criminals. Police and military crackdown was outrageous, provocative, and violent.

Fin was used to violence, but his life's interior had changed. After a day's work making deliveries in Dublin, he retreated home to the room he shared with Fionaghalla and their son, Cormac. The room was a mildewed box on a dismal street, but this made Fionaghalla and Cormac's presences all the more compelling to Fin. Cormac was two and a half. His talk mimicked Fin's, as his watchfulness did his mother's, and he looked like Fin, if healthier, but his exuberance was wholly his own.

Like Fin, the child called the mute woman Fionaghalla— Finella. Keyed to her through infancy's own muteness, Cormac could translate her moods and gestures even better than could Fin, but Fionaghalla's silence rarely frustrated

Fin. He rested in it, saline, buoying him without promise or artifice or agenda. His heart cleared, and his body eased. He asked no explanation of her, knowing none could be given, but took her in sudden, fierce couplings that left him as weak and invincible as a drunk. Her hands skimmed the scars of his body, reading him; her mouth opened under his; her limbs twined him, grip and release, tides that, receding, had revealed the humbling rise of her pregnancy.

When Cormac was born, Fionaghalla left the waterfront job Fin had gotten her and never returned to it. She tucked Cormac into a shawl sling on her back and spent her days foraging on the shore. She foraged at lochs and burns, too; she poached fish and snared rabbits and birds, gathered wild plants and seaweed, and, Fin suspected, stole vegetables and fruits from gardens she passed on those forays. She went rural-proud, her herring *cutlag* at her waist. Seeing her, the silence like midnight at noon, people did not prevent or forget her.

Fin grew careless of himself and protective of mother and child, though realized Fionaghalla could not be made safe; it was not unlike his own danger as part of the IRB: she lived outside forgiveness.

One Sunday in August they went to the shore, all three on Fin's bicycle. He fell asleep in the warmth, head on his coat, and when he woke with his usual instant alertness, Cormac and Fionaghalla were nowhere to be seen. Thinking they had wandered down to the shore, the boy learning from his mother's example the mysteries of mussels, crabs, things that could be eaten and things that could not, Fin sat on a rock and gazed out to sea. He was not an introspective man, though knew himself; nor was he a sailor or fisherman. His family ever had turned their faces inland to the cattle, the fire-hearted horses, the crops. Mayo: poor and boggy and bare. He did and did not miss it here in Dublin, a city founded by Vikings, still lacking a rooted Irish soul.

As Fin gazed, thinking on Mayo, he realized there was something moving in the water. He stood to see better, then climbed atop the stone for a more advantageous view. He stared. It was Fionaghalla, Cormac upon her naked breast, floating like seals on the cold swells of the Irish Sea.

He was speechless, then wanted to shout but did not. Impulse, borne of fright and yearning, died in the tightness of his chest. He closed his eyes and bowed his head, stepping down from the rock, standing unmoving until Fionaghalla walked naked from the sea, Cormac in her arms, her long hair streaming.

"Do not ever take him so far into the sea again," Fin said that night when they were in bed. "Do not." He rolled atop her, hands pinning hers on either side of her head, and licked the salty hollow of her throat, kissed her mouth, slid lower to suck the round breasts, tasting the sea on all of her. He raised himself and entered her, felt her shudder as though harpooned. He let go of her hands, but she did not move them.

"Fionaghalla." The fear he'd felt on the shore again was upon him. He froze, lust driving him, but he held motionless, restraint that could only be self-imposed. He whispered her name, speaking to her in liquid Gaelic, and, after a time, she slipped her arms around his neck and softened her body to his thrusts.

Fin slept and dreamed. In the morning, waking to find himself alone with Cormac, he wept, knowing he would never see her again.

Chris Docherty came into the hostel laundry room to use the iron, as Trinity was pulling clothes from the dryer. He nodded to her, unlimbering the ironing board with a shriek of metal joints, and smoothed a white shirt over one end.

Trinity began folding one of her own shirts. "Date tonight?" she asked, as the Irishman set to his task.

"Mebbe."

She finished folding the shirt, started on another. "Tell me, if you would—though I'm not assuming that you know—"she said, somewhere between a mumble and a blurt, "why the timing? Why did Rory and Connell do what they did right before the ceasefire for the peace talks? Were they trying to sabotage the peace process?"

Chris neatly poked the tip of the iron along the points of his shirt collar, glanced up, and gave her a hostile look. "No, they weren't trying to sabotage the talks. I'm not involved with that shite, but obviously, their aim was to escalate pressure on the Brits." He moved the iron and began erasing wrinkles from the sleeves.

"You're very good at that," Trinity observed, placating.

He thumped the iron onto its base, adjusted the shirt's position, then glided the iron over the shirt back. "You want to know about Connell O'Sullivan and me?" The placation hadn't worked. "We went to school together. My sister, Eileen, dated Connell and married him in 1974. She was only nineteen. So was he, but already a known Provo. It was obligatory in his family: IRB, IRA, whatever. His father was a major player, like his grandfather and on up. Anyway, five months after the wedding, Eileen was dead—pregnant and dead."

"What happened?" she finally asked.

"Crossfire. The bad, bad seventies." He glanced up at her silence, yanked the plug on the iron, picked up his immaculate shirt, and left.

Trinity stopped working on the selkie tale, putting it aside like a dream that needs to be ignored in order to be recalled. Instead, she applied herself to paperwork for the Ferinurchar proposal, finishing during the last of the heather's bloom, hiking over the boggy moor to Kilmuir one Sunday, rucksack filled with papers.

She found Alie at home, just in from busking at Duntulm, still wearing his kilt.

"You're fast," he said, when she began unloading her pack onto his table.

"There were no other demands on my time," she said drily.

He stood, looking down at the tidy stack of papers; she'd returned all the materials he'd given her, plus the completed proposals. "Thanks," he said. "This is brilliant."

"You haven't read it yet," she protested. "I might've gotten it all wrong."

Alie shook his head. "Not you."

She turned away, went to the window. The sun was beginning its slow plunge toward the Western Isles.

"You're leaving Scotland soon, aren't you?" An accusation.

Trinity shrugged.

"Missing the States?"

"No."

"You'd do all right here."

She faced him. "I hope to come back and find you and the others making a future at Ferinurchar. You'll let me know how things turn out? I'll give you my e-mail address."

"Of course I'll let you know." He watched while she jotted the address and set down the pen. "Let's go outside. I'll give you a tune before you go." He bent to one of the open cases and lifted a low whistle, then led her outside. "Highland music is always best outdoors, even with the midges."

Trinity sat on a stone, a pouring wind carrying off the midges, the notes of *Calum's Cattle* singing over the moor.

It was dark when she arrived back at the hostel. She entered the dining room with its clatter and conversation, and set her rucksack beside a chair. She was hungry but sat down, a tiredness that needed transition between walking and eating, between the timeless dark moor and modernity's bright countenance.

She noticed Chris when his proximity demanded her attention.

"Did you hear?" he asked, can of lager in one hand, an unlit roll-up in the other.

"Hear what?"

He shook his head in disgust. "Jesus God. Do you never listen to the news?"

"Hear what?" she demanded, dread's agitation.

Chris glanced around, congenital Irish discretion. "Come on. Not in here," he said with a tight jerk of his blond head toward the door. "I need my fag."

They sat atop one of the picnic tables, feet on the bench. Chris offered her his beer—she took a sip and handed it back, then took the cigarette from between his nicotined fingers and drew on it, returning it. "So tell me."

"They're giving amnesty to IRA prisoners, part of the Good Friday agreement. They're releasing them from Long Kesh this week."

"Letting them out? All of them?"

Chris sighed at her sluggish uptake. "Aye." He drank his lager, smoked.

"When? This week?"

"This week."

The moon had risen over Staffin Bay, its wealth glimmering on the waves. The world's oldest language, cold fire on the dark sea, the secret known by every cell.

Chris tossed his cigarette into the dewy grass. "My job here finishes at the end of the month." He turned to her with the patience offered the dense. "That's this week."

Trinity nodded.

Chris sighed again, long-suffering. "So. Will you be wanting a ride to Belfast?"

Light on water, the ten thousand shifting thresholds fracturing, eternally reappearing.

THE SELKIE'S LINEAGE

Trinity smiled.

EPILOGUE

Fin O'Sullivan continued to live in Dublin, active in the IRB until his death from tuberculosis in 1897. His son, Cormac, Connell's great-grandfather, was killed at age thirty-two during the 1916 Easter Uprising in Dublin.

Margaret Ross MacKinnon returned to Braes after a visit to her nephew Murdoch's wife in Canada. She outlived her husband, Angus, by many years, well beloved in her township for her stories, her strong spirit, and her fidelity to the cause of justice for Gaels.

Trinity's great-grandfather, Duncan Ross, was born in Nova Scotia two months after his father's drowning in 1887. He lived and died a fisherman and was one of Cape Breton's finest fiddlers.

Michael Davitt continued his efforts on behalf of the working class: he founded the Irish Democratic and Trade, and the Labour Federation. In 1895, he was elected MP for South Mayo and served in the House of Commons for four years, where his chief concerns were prison reform and social justice. He resigned his parliamentary seat in protest of the Boer War.

In Davitt's last will, he wrote: To all my friends I leave kind thoughts; to my enemies, my fullest possible forgiveness; and to Ireland, my undying prayer for the absolute freedom and independence which it was my life's ambition to try and obtain for her.

THE SELKIE'S LINEAGE

The Selkie's Lineage

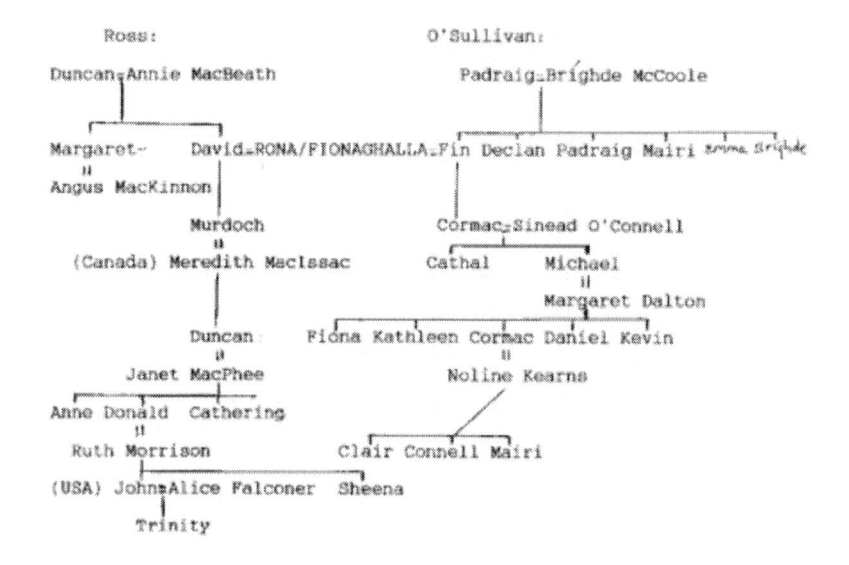

```
Ross:                                    O'Sullivan:
Duncan=Annie MacBeath                    Padraig=Bríghde McCoole
       |                                        |
┌──────┴──────┐                    ┌────┬───┬───┴──┬────────┬──────┐
Margaret-  David=RONA/FIONAGHALLA=Fin  Declan Padraig Mairi Anna Bríghde
    ii                             |
Angus MacKinnon                    |
       |                           |
       Murdoch                     Cormac=Sinead O'Connell
          ii                          ┌─────┴─────┐
(Canada) Meredith MacIssac           Cathal     Michael
       |                                           ii
       |                                    Margaret Dalton
       Duncan:        Fiona Kathleen Cormac Daniel Kevin
           ii                              ii
       Janet MacPhee                  Noline Kearns
   ┌───────┬────────┐
Anne Donald  Cathering
         ii
   Ruth Morrison         Clair Connell Mairi
       ┌──────┴──────┐
(USA) John=Alice Falconer  Sheena
         |
       Trinity
```

128

ACTUAL/HISTORICAL FIGURES APPEARING IN THE SELKIE'S LINEAGE:

PART ONE

Sheriff Donald MacLeod

The Black Watch

Reverend Alexander MacBean

William Robertson

James Falconer Gillanders

John Chisholm

Gustavus Aird

Alexander Munro

Sheriff-substitute Taylor

Christy Ross

Elizabeth Ross

Janet Ross

Margaret Ross (2)

Ann Munro

Grace Ross

Naomi Ross

Catherine Ross

Donald Ross

Osgood MacKenzie

Mary MacKenzie

Hugh MacLean

Duncan MacKenzie

Roddy MacKenzie

Dr. John MacKenzie

PART TWO

Michael Davitt—Ireland

John Murdoch

Charles Stuart Parnell—Ireland

Thomas Daly—Ireland

John Bourke—Ireland

John Ferguson—Ireland

O'Connor Power—Ireland

Thomas Brennan—Ireland

Andrew Conneely—Ireland

Mrs. Maickle—Ireland

Alexander MacDonald

Captain William Fraser

Lord MacDonald

Captain Charles Boycott—Ireland

Lord Erne—Ireland

Father O'Malley—Ireland

James Redpath—USA

Anna Parnell—Ireland

John Dillon—Ireland

Prime Minister Gladstone—England

Mrs. Mary Deane—Ireland

Ellen McDonagh—Ireland

Patrick Melody—Ireland

John Macpherson

Reverend McRae

Angus Martin

THE SELKIE'S LINEAGE

Ewan Robertson

Norman Beaton

John Nicolson

Mairi nic Phuilaidh

Marion MacMillan

Sheriff Ivory

Secretary Forster—England

Lord Cavandish—Ireland

Reverend Donald MacCallum

Sir William Harcourt—England

D. H. MacFarlane

Kitty O'Shea—Ireland

Lord Napier

MacKenzie of Gairloch

Cameron of Lochiel

Fraser MacIntosh

Professor MacKinnon

Sheriff Nicolson

Chief Constable McHardy

The sacked crew of the *Lochiel*

John MacKay

Mary Yore—Ireland

Marines, police, and other unnamed military, law enforcement, and judicial figures

PARTIAL BIBLIOGRAPHY

Devine, T.M. *Clanship to Crofter's War: The Social Transformation of the Scottish Highlands.* Manchester: Manchester University Press, 1994.

Grant, I. F. *Highland Folk Ways.* London: Routledge, 1961.

Hunter, James. *The Making of the Crofting Community.* Edinburgh: John MacDonald Publishing, 1976.

MacKenzie, Alexander. *History of the Highland Clearances.* London: Melvin, 1986.

MacManus, Seamus. The *Story of the Irish R*ace. New York: Devin-Adair, 1944.

MacPhail, I.M.M. *The Crofter's War.* Stornoway: Acair, 1989.

Macpherson, George W. *John Macpherson, The Skye Martyr.* Isle of Skye: West Highland Publishing, 1995.

Newton, Michael. *Handbook of the Scottish Gaelic World.* Portland: Four Courts Press, 2000.

Nicolson, Alexander. *History of Skye: A Record of the Families, The Social Conditions, and The Literature of the Island.* Portree: MacLean Press, 1994.

Prebble, John. *The Highland Clearances*. London: Penguin, 1969.

Richards, Eric. *A History of the Highland Clearances*. London: Croom Helm, 1982.

Ross, Anne. *Folklore of the Scottish Highlands*. New York: Barnes & Noble, 1976.

Taylor, Peter. *Behind the Mask: The IRA and the Sinn Fein*. New York: TV Books, 1997.

Miscellaneous archive material, including: *Gairloch and Guide to Loch Maree* and *Peoples and Settlement in North-West Ross*, and letters and documents in the Michael Davitt Museum.

THE AUTHOR

Other books by Loren Cruden:

Nonfiction:
- *The Spirit of Place*
- *Coyote's Council Fire*
- *Compass of the Heart*
- *Medicine Grove*
- *Walking the Maze*
- *Eating Diamonds*
- *Aware Practice*
- *Circular Time*

Fiction:
- *Debatable Lands*

For workshops, Loren can be contacted at:
P.O. Box 218, Orient, WA 99160.

Cover and author photos by Gabriel Cruden

Printed in Great Britain
by Amazon.co.uk, Ltd.,
Marston Gate.